THE UNEXPECTED TALE
of
BASTIEN
BON LIVRE

To Mum and Dad, for their unconditional love
and support

To Adam, for making every day unexpected
in the best possible way

First published in the UK in 2021 by Usborne Publishing Ltd., Usborne House,
83-85 Saffron Hill, London EC1N 8RT, England. usborne.com

Usborne Verlag, Usborne Publishing Ltd., Prüfeninger Str. 20, 93049 Regensburg,
Deutschland VK Nr. 17560

Text © Clare Povey, 2021.

Cover and inside illustrations, including map by Héloïse Mab ©
Usborne Publishing, 2021.

Typography by Thy Bui © Usborne Publishing, 2021.

The right of Clare Povey to be identified as the author of this work has been asserted by
her in accordance with the Copyright, Designs and Patents Act, 1988.

The name Usborne and the Balloon logos are Trade Marks of Usborne Publishing Ltd.

A CIP catalogue record for this book is available from the British Library.

ISBN 9781474986489   05997/3 JFMAMJJ SOND/21

Printed and bound in Great Britain by CPI Group (UK) Ltd, Croydon, CR0 4YY.

THE UNEXPECTED TALE

of

BASTIEN

BON LIVRE

CLARE POVEY

USBORNE

CONTENTS

BASTIEN'S MAP OF PARIS,
1922

Grand Palais

Eiffel Tower

Le Chat Curieux

Olivier's house

Le Malheur

Sacré-Coeur

Gare du Nord

Ritz Hotel

Le Louvre

Notre-Dame

Les Catacombes

Gare de Lyon

Orphanage

Le Parisien

JEUDI, 31 AOÛT 1922

AUTHORS PERISH IN

Celebrated writers Margot and Hugo Bonlivre tragically died last night in a fire at the InterContinental Carlton Hôtel, just hours before they were due to be welcomed as guests of honour at the Cannes Book Festival.

Margot and Hugo will be best remembered for their very first novel written together ten years ago: *The Voyage to the Edge of the Sky.* Though the two authors received some acclaim for their individual works, it was their joint book that became an international bestseller and firmly cemented their place as two of the most successful storytellers in Europe.

The news of their lives being cut so suddenly short will send shockwaves through the world. Authorities are investigating and witness interviews are under way to confirm how the fire started on the hotel's tenth floor. Police are keen to speak to all those who were residents of the hotel at the time of the incident, especially anyone who was staying on the same floor. According to an anonymous hotel worker, who this newspaper

Quotidien

PRIX:
0 FR.30

60, RUE LA FAYETTE

TRAGIC HOTEL BLAZE

spoke with exclusively, a dark-haired man and a young American couple were booked into the rooms opposite the Bonlivres'.

Margot and Hugo Bonlivre had been due to give a speech at the festival dinner yesterday evening. People from all over the continent had gathered in Cannes to attend, as it was understood the couple were intending to make an announcement. Whether it was about a new book or something entirely different, we can only guess.

The couple leave behind their only child, Bastien, aged twelve. At the time of his parents' death, Bastien was staying with Jules and Charlotte Delacroix, owners of Le Chat Curieux bookshop on the left bank of the Seine.

With no immediate family in Paris and any remaining relatives unknown, Bastien will be sent to the city orphanage for boys and will live there until he is eighteen.

Writers all over the world will weep this morning. Not only for the loss of two of our brightest minds, but for all the words they had yet to write. ■

1

UP IN FLAMES

Winter arrived in Paris on a November evening, later than expected, and Bastien realized he was in trouble. He looked around the dormitory as the metal beds of the other boys creaked from the weight of the bitter wind. Snores floated through the air, for they were all fast asleep apart from him. An urge to write had kept him up long past bedtime, despite the cold and frosty Parisian winter that could eat into brains like rot. Bastien shivered; he had to get out of here.

"Here" was the Orphanage for Gentils Garçons in the Petit-Montrouge neighbourhood, where Bastien had lived for the last three months.

Since the day the police had told him of his parents'

fate, happiness had drained out of Bastien like a slow gas leak. With no other existing family to turn to, the authorities had marched him across the river and through the doors of his new home.

He had not gone willingly.

When Bastien was old enough to understand words, his father had named their family The Three Musketeers, for they were united in strength, spirit and look. Bastien had the same fair hair and topaz-coloured eyes as his parents. The freckles that ran across his face and down his arms were an exact reflection of his mother's, and he'd always asked the barber to cut his hair short, just like his father's. The three of them had never needed anyone else, for they had each other.

Now, under the charge of Monsieur Xavier – the new orphanage director who cared for the boys as much as a pickpocket cared for an honest living – Bastien prayed nightly for a long-lost great-aunt to burst through the doors and save him from the misery of scrubbing toilet bowls.

But tonight was not that night.

Bastien looked over at the low, flickering flames of the furnace in the middle of the dormitory. It was the only light in the dark room. Metal beds were lined up in uniform rows either side of it, one each for the eight boys who currently lived here, destined to spend the rest of their days together until they turned eighteen.

The brick walls were bare, apart from a single, barred window and an old painting of dark-brown eyes that hung on the far wall. Felix, one of the other boys, had sworn he'd seen the eyes blink before.

Bastien rubbed his hands together, warming his fingers, which felt as frozen as icicles. He slipped out from his blanket and placed his pocket-sized notebook beneath the loose floorboard under his bed. If he was caught writing after dark in a notebook he wasn't supposed to have, there'd be a heavy price to pay. Stories were strictly forbidden.

Monsieur Xavier had arrived only days after Bastien and enforced his harsh rules without pausing for breath. The boys all missed the old director; the kind-hearted Monsieur Dupont, who'd gone for a walk along the river Seine early one morning and never returned. He'd treated them with compassion, whereas Monsieur Xavier had swept in like a bad smell and proceeded to empty all of the boys' trunks, telling them that their personal belongings would need to be sold off to provide enough money for their keep.

Sensing Monsieur Xavier's cruelty, Bastien had hidden, under the loose floorboard, the few belongings he'd managed to rescue from home: a copy of his parents' book, *The Voyage to the Edge of the Sky*, as well as his burgundy leather pocket notebook and pen. He would never part with them; they were all he had from his previous life.

The notebook had been a gift from his parents the night before they'd left for Cannes that summer. They'd bought many notebooks for him to write in before, but this one was different. Inside was blank, apart from the first line of a story they'd written: "*Once upon a time, there were three musketeers destined for a great adventure.*"

"This tale starts with us, but it ends with you," his mother had said as she passed him the gift across the table.

"Go forward and write the unexpected." His father had paused, taken Bastien's hand and clutched it tightly in his own. "Keep this notebook safe and never let it fall into the wrong hands. This is your story to tell."

Bastien had looked curiously at his father, who was usually joyful and as light as the paper he wrote on. The serious look on his face didn't suit him and so Bastien had smiled and hugged him tightly, almost knocking over the bowl of lemon juice for their crêpes.

"Promise," Bastien had replied.

Bastien had kept this promise and always kept his notebook close, but tonight had been the first time since the summer that he'd felt the urge to pick up a pen. He'd been too sad. How could he write without his parents? He was supposed to tell stories about their endless adventures, but now they were gone and he was stuck here.

He still didn't understand how it had happened, how a fire had broken out in the finest hotel in all of Cannes and taken his parents away from him in a matter of minutes. Bastien was supposed to accept it, but what if he didn't want to? He just wanted them back.

Still, he was a Bonlivre. He knew that meant something. Even though the four brick walls of the orphanage stunted his ideas – every new seed of a story wilting before it had a chance to truly grow – Bastien reread *The Voyage to the Edge of the Sky* most nights under his blanket, with the hope that his parents' magical words might rub off on him.

Before, Bastien had always walked around with a book permanently glued to his nose. Limiting what he read was like asking the roses in the Luxembourg Gardens not to grow: it was simply against his nature.

The locked doors that kept the boys trapped inside, away from Paris, were another reminder of the bleakness of a place he could never call home. Monsieur Xavier dictated their every waking moment, but Bastien noticed how the director's coal-black eyes always lingered on him for longer than anyone else.

How he missed the freedom to roam his city! Bastien missed morning games of hopscotch outside his apartment with the neighbourhood kids. He missed weekend adventures with his parents; taking the train north to Lille or going on long walks in the Forest of Fontainebleau and climbing to the top of the gorge.

Most of all, Bastien missed Le Chat Curieux. It was his favourite bookshop on the left bank of the Seine, owned by Charlotte and Jules Delacroix. He'd first visited with his parents when he was barely old enough to walk, but he'd stumbled through the door and made a firm friend in Alice, Charlotte and Jules's daughter. Bastien missed her terribly. He often wondered why she hadn't visited or written yet, like she'd promised. Had she already forgotten all about him?

Bastien had pleaded with Jules and Charlotte to take

a
muc...
was not t...
dormitory ro...
that his dreams ...
grand fantasies, and ...
finishing the story in his n...
or being happy – *truly* happy –

The heavy thud of the double dormitory doors quickly pulled Bastien from his reverie. The creeping footsteps of Monsieur Xavier approached for the routine midnight inspection and Bastien watched from back under his blanket as the man came to a stop in front of the furnace.

Although the director cared very little for the boys, he drew the line at letting them all perish of pneumonia, for if he didn't keep them alive and well he wouldn't receive any money from the government. For Monsieur Xavier, a life without luxury was unimaginable; the greatest tragedy at the orphanage wouldn't be an outbreak of tuberculosis, but a lack of fresh oysters for his dinner.

coal next to
out and upside down.
umbs and the director's grumble
the walls.

Bastien wondered if any of the other boys were
awake; the director's leather boots slapped loudly on
the floor and were impossible to ignore. If they were, no
one dared to move. Last month when Monsieur Xavier
was carrying out his nightly inspection, Timothée, one
of the older boys, had risked a trip to the toilet after a
few secret sips of apple juice that Chef had snuck into
the dormitory. Timothée had ended up without a
blanket to sleep under for a week; to be without one this
winter didn't bear thinking about.

Eventually, the sound of footsteps faded into nothing
and Bastien's relief floated up like a kite. He rolled over
on his side and realized his relief had been too quick.
Monsieur Xavier's hot-anchovy breath lingered in the
air and Bastien squeezed his eyes shut so hard that black
rings swallowed the director. All fell quiet, except for
the sound of fingernails scraping.

Although he knew he shouldn't – for a look risked
too much – he dared to open one eye.

What Bastien saw next made him cry out in pain

as though he'd been struck in the face.

The Voyage to the Edge of the Sky was in Monsieur Xavier's hands and he was headed for the furnace.

THE ISOLATION CHAMBER

Instinct pulled Bastien from his bed. How had he been so careless as to not hide his parents' book properly? He'd been too distracted with his own writing and left it to get tangled in the ends of his blanket.

The shock of the cold wooden floor on his bare feet made him catch his breath, but his rage was a fever: aching and burning.

"Give that back! I won't let you burn it!" Bastien threw himself at his book.

"What do you think you are doing, you horrible little beast?" Monsieur Xavier's long pointed face turned red with rage. He ripped the book away from Bastien's weak grip; the result of eating watered-down soups and bowls of mushy vegetables for dinner.

"Taking back what's mine," Bastien cried.

"You know by now not to be out of bed at this hour." Flecks of spittle flew from Monsieur Xavier's mouth. "And you certainly get no say in what I do with this book you've been hiding. Despicable."

"But, but…" Bastien muttered. "That was from home."

Mutters and grunts echoed around the dormitory. Some of the others were sat up in their beds, faces wild with horror. Robin pulled his blanket up over his eyes and Pascal muttered a quiet prayer under his breath. The twins Felix and Fred were still fast asleep; the commotion lost in the sound of their own snores.

Monsieur Xavier took another step closer, towering over Bastien. His shiny, black hair dangled in clumps and his forehead bulged with angry veins. "You don't have a home any more." The director's laugh burst from the pit of his stomach, revealing rows of chipped, yellowing teeth and a cracked tongue. "It is long gone. Just like your parents."

"Don't you *ever* talk about my parents!"

Monsieur Xavier didn't reply. He walked over to the furnace, his floor-length black cloak swishing behind him, and, with a simple flick of his wrist, threw the book into the fire.

Bastien ran towards the flames, but it was too late. The fire roared and he watched his book burn to blackened ash. It brought him to his knees.

"Bastien, let it go," a familiar voice whispered. It was Theo, his closest friend. He'd been at the orphanage a month longer than Bastien, but they'd got on instantly, as though they'd been friends for ever.

"Theo!" Monsieur Xavier called. "Back to bed, otherwise it'll be your blanket in the furnace next."

Theo bravely ignored the threat and crept forward, his small, quick frame darting through the dim dormitory. Bastien felt Theo's hand on his back, as the boy helped to pull him up onto his feet.

"That was my parents' book." Sadness dripped from each of his words. "It was my only copy."

"You carry your mother and father with you each day," Theo replied. "They're always with you in heart and mind. *Toujours*."

Theo was a year younger than Bastien but he was definitely the wisest person in the orphanage, Monsieur Xavier included. The director had confiscated Theo's silver brooch the week before; it had belonged to his mother and had been crafted in her home of Ath Yenni, in the northern mountains of Algeria. Bastien had felt the gravity of Theo's loss then, as his friend did now. They helped each other through the hard times.

If it hadn't been for Monsieur Xavier's lingering presence – his beady eyes tracking Bastien's every move, like a hawk about to claim its prey, Bastien would've felt comforted by Theo's words.

"Come along, Bastien." Monsieur Xavier outstretched his bony hand. "The Isolation Chamber awaits."

Bastien's entire body flinched. He ignored Monsieur Xavier and walked back towards his bed, but the director had other ideas. His large hands swooped down onto Bastien's shoulders like metal clamps.

"Did you really think you could get away with backchat? And hiding a contraband item? No, no, that won't do at all, *petit chenapan*. You shall be punished accordingly."

Bastien wished the solid ground beneath his feet would turn to quicksand and pull him under. He'd never spent a night in the Isolation Chamber, but the rumours he'd heard of it – of boys fighting rats as large as cats in there – were more frightening than any nightmare. It was a place so small you could only stand. It was a place

25

where time didn't exist because it was always pitch-black. It was a place every single boy feared.

Bastien was marched out of the dormitory, catching a glimpse of Theo looking on helplessly as the doors slammed shut and locked with a hissing click. Monsieur Xavier directed him to the end of the corridor, passing the staircases and stopping just short of the east wing. To the right was a thin wooden door, rusting badly at its hinges with protruding nails hanging from the frame. Bastien protested but he was too weak; he had no fight left.

"In you go." The director pulled the door open and pushed Bastien into a darkness that enveloped him. "I'll be back to let you out in nine hours. If you behave."

"Do you have a blanket?" Bastien's skin was already turning to gooseflesh. *"S'il vous plaît."*

Monsieur Xavier smirked. His face, illuminated by the burning oil lamps in the corridor, was a picture of pure delight and Bastien knew that the man would never take pity on him.

"Blankets are for boys who don't talk back. Sleep poorly, Bastien." The door closed and a key turned slowly in the stiff lock. Only the low laughter of the director could be heard before a disturbing silence fell over the orphanage.

Bastien closed his eyes. It didn't make any difference, for even with them open it was still impossible to see. He hit his head against the wall as he tried to sit down. The hours until morning would feel twice as long if he had to stand all night.

His hands landed upon something rough and scratchy and he jumped back in fright. What else was in here? He felt about in the dark, his tongue between his teeth, as he slowly lowered himself down to the floor. The smallest sliver of light creeping in from the bottom of the door illuminated the bristles of a broom right next to him.

So, the feared Isolation Chamber was nothing more than a cleaning cupboard! Bastien wanted to laugh, but it caught in his throat.

How had he gone from a happy, loving life with his parents to this? He scrunched his eyes tighter and wished for a kernel of a story idea to pop, anything to distract himself, but nothing came. His ideas had abandoned him, squeezed from his brain by the orphanage and its strict rules. He wasn't much without a story simmering away inside of him. Half-crouching, half-sitting in a broom cupboard, his imagination admitted defeat. But only for tonight.

Bastien wasn't going to stay locked up for ever. There were still adventures to be had – maybe a different kind from what he'd imagined before the fire, but a life to live all the same. His tale was only just beginning and he wasn't about to let Monsieur Xavier decide how it would end.

It was that thought which gently lulled Bastien into an uncomfortable sleep.

AN UNEXPECTED ESCAPE

That night, all Bastien could dream about was his old life. He clung onto the cliff edge of his past. For ten years, he'd lived on the fourth floor of an old apartment block in Belleville, north-east of the city centre. His parents had bought the apartment after their first book together had sold all around the world. It hadn't been the most expensive of purchases, but for Bastien's parents, who'd sprung from humble roots in the outskirts of the city, the northern *banlieues* of Paris, it was an indulgence as rich as chocolate gâteau.

There had been three bedrooms: one for his parents, one for Bastien and one for their books. His mother always said that books deserved their proper place, for they held the power to change the world itself. Books didn't appreciate being stored in cardboard boxes, collecting dust and their pages yellowing. So, they got a room all to themselves. Naturally, it was Bastien's favourite room and he'd spent more time there than in his own bedroom.

They would eat breakfast on the balcony each morning, before Bastien left for school. With a milky *chocolat chaud* in his hand, which he drank even in the height of summer, Bastien would look out at the rolling hills of the neighbourhood park and the sprawling views of the city below. He was happy to become part of the skyline, a small figure lost to the rooftops. Somewhere among the stepping stones of buildings, cathedral spires and the glimmer of the Eiffel Tower in the distance, Bastien's imagination would spring alive with stories that propelled him back to his bedroom desk with the speed of a race car. His father often had to drag him away so he wouldn't be late for school.

In the evenings, Bastien told tales to his neighbours, and the other children listened in awe. He dreamed of such evenings now; he would do anything to get them back.

The next morning, after Monsieur Xavier had finally let him out of the Isolation Chamber, Bastien joined Theo in the courtyard to sweep away the first smatterings of snow. His brain was so empty, his body so numb from the cold, that he worried his imagination had fallen out of his ear. He yawned, rubbing his neck and cracking his knuckles. The chamber had cramped his bones and he longed for a rest, yet he continued to sweep. He had no choice.

Theo noticed the faraway look in Bastien's eyes.

"Your stories will return," Theo said, sitting down on the courtyard steps. He took off his skin-coloured gloves, made from sandy beige fabric, and carefully folded them into his pocket. Gloves were a luxury the director considered unnecessary for such unworthy boys, but Theo knew their hands wouldn't survive the winter without them. He'd made pairs for all the boys in their own skin tones, using scraps of different material stolen from the curtains Monsieur Xavier had torn down in every room. If the director noticed, he would surely confiscate them.

"How can you be sure?" Bastien sat beside him.

"When you're not thinking about it, they will come back. Each story will walk right back up to your brain and knock on the door." Theo rapped his knuckles against Bastien's forehead.

"I hope you're right," Bastien replied, swallowing a laugh. "It's hard to find inspiration in this miserable place."

The orphanage had once been a smart-looking building with Monsieur Dupont at the helm. There had been a perfectly-pruned courtyard, colourful tiles, feather quilts and sparkling silver cutlery at dinnertime. But it had quickly fallen into disrepair under Monsieur Xavier's watch. Where there had once been life, there was now decay. Broken glass panels covered the face of the grey-stone building and loose tiles fell from the roof as often as rain. The director had cut down the apple trees in the courtyard and replaced the old curtains with thick black ones over every window.

"I know." Theo's green eyes sparkled with mischief. "Misery is in Monsieur Xavier's blood."

As if on cue, a hacking cough sounded behind them. Monsieur Xavier always miraculously seemed to show up as soon as they started talking about him.

"Get back to work, you termites!" His voice was hard and sharp, a knife's edge. "It'll be another night of sleeping with the rats if you ignore me." With an exasperated sigh, he turned back inside and slammed the door shut.

Bastien and Theo reluctantly got back up on their feet, brooms in hand. Today, they were the only two on courtyard duties. Still, Bastien was thankful for the broom; it kept him upright when all he wanted to do was curl up and sleep.

"Any chance you could invent an automatic sweeper?" Bastien yawned.

Theo's parents had been inventors and he'd inherited their knack for creating brilliant things out of the most basic of materials. His mother had made fine, fantastical jewellery with nothing more than melted scraps of silver, and his father had always been looking for new ways to keep his feet firmly off the ground, inventing flying machines of every type. They'd lost their lives in a blimp experiment gone wrong and a dizzying fear of heights was all that had saved Theo from joining them. His father's pressure calculations had been off by the slightest of fractions on his new airship – a simple error that had cost them their lives.

Tools were limited in the orphanage, but where others saw broken parts and old scraps, Theo saw fully-formed objects. He'd even fashioned Bastien a reading light out of a candle stump, an old glass jar, some string and a box of matches pilfered from Chef's cupboards.

"I'll get to work on it." Theo smiled. "Although sweeping did lead me to find plenty of this over by the fountain." From his pocket he pulled a lump of green moss. "I'm going to make earmuffs with it for everyone. I haven't had a decent night's sleep since I got here. Felix and Fred's snoring is as loud as a foghorn!"

Bastien groaned in sympathy. "They even snore at the same frequency. I can't take much more."

Theo shrugged. "Must be a twin thing."

Sweeping the rest of the courtyard didn't take long, but Bastien dragged out each minute until they doubled, battling through his yawns. After a night plunged in darkness, he wanted to soak up every last bit of light until he was forced to return back inside.

When the rest of the daily chores were done, which included delights such as scrubbing the bathroom floor and helping Chef peel onions in the kitchen, Bastien took his seat in the dining hall. Life at the orphanage repeated itself like a broken film on a projector, and Bastien hated the predictability of each day. The boys all sat crammed on a bench along a wooden table, their elbows knocking into each other as they ate.

Theo sat next to him, eyeing the food on his plate as if it was his last meal before the guillotine. Bastien, on the other hand, thought that removing his own taste buds was a better option than eating another orphanage dinner, even if he was as hungry as a wolf.

"What *un*delightful dish do we have tonight then?" Pascal called from the top of the bench, quietly enough for only the boys to hear. Pascal's father had been a cook during the war and the boy had inherited his love of food and smell. He leaned forward, his short, wide nose trying to locate an aroma.

Timothée threw his spoon down in outrage. "This isn't food, this is a drink!" He dipped his finger in the puddle on his plate and used the liquid to slick back his thick, black hair. The world was Timothée's stage and he was always looking for new ways to be the centre of attention. "Whatever it is, it works well for hair styling, though."

Bastien watched, with two parts disgust and one part strange admiration, as Theo chewed down tonight's offering: onion soup, which was in fact just chopped chunks of mostly raw onions mixed with a dribble of tap water, and a slice of baguette as hard as a police baton.

On the other side of him sat a boy that Bastien still knew little about. Sami was neck-achingly tall, with shoulders as wide as the river Seine and honey-coloured eyes that observed everything around him. No one knew Sami's age, but the tufts of dark hair that grew in patches on his face like untamed weeds confirmed he was the oldest boy at the orphanage.

Sami had arrived earlier that summer, and had never said a single word to anyone. His bed was right next to Bastien's and on some nights he sang in his sleep. Bastien recognized the melodies as malhun, beautiful sung poetry from Morocco. Bastien's father had had a friend called Driss, who'd come from the North African country and was forced to fight in the war. He'd visited them in Paris many times and Bastien had always loved swapping stories with him. After dinner, Bastien would curl up next to his parents as they listened to Driss sing the familiar tunes that Sami now muttered in his dreams.

Bastien wondered what had happened for Sami to end up in the most miserable orphanage in France.

Sami's head whipped around and Bastien realized

he'd been staring for longer than was polite. The older boy's stare burned into Bastien's skin and, feeling embarrassed, he stuttered out an apology before turning around. He didn't want to make another enemy; dealing with Monsieur Xavier was challenging enough.

"Are you going to eat that?"

Bastien somehow understood Theo's words through a spray of crumbs and pushed his plate towards him.

"Help yourself."

Theo received the plate with eager hands and slurped down the watery onion mixture.

"I miss Yemma's *mchawcha*." Theo licked his lips.

"What's that?" Bastien sipped at a chipped mug of sour milk.

"A sweet, sugary type of omelette with lashings of honey. It's the most delicious thing you could ever hope to eat. Not like this rubbish." Theo hit the baguette on the table; the bread survived unscathed but left a small dent on the table's surface. Nonetheless, he sank his teeth into the rock-hard dough. There wasn't much Theo refused to eat. Only last week he'd chipped his front tooth trying to eat a whole mussel, the shell still intact.

"When we get out of here, we'll eat until our bellies

are bursting." He patted his stomach as though it was full.

"As long as we can go to the sweet shop near the Trocadéro for dessert," Bastien replied, dreaming of all the delicious bonbons he used to eat on weekend afternoons. He could almost taste the sharp tang of lemon sherbet and melt-in-your-mouth salted butter caramels.

Bastien and Theo looked over to the table at the far end of the dining hall where Monsieur Xavier sat, surrounded by large silver plates of food. There was an entire roast duck, glistening in an orange glow, alongside lashings of dauphinoise potatoes and golden-coloured frites. Chef, an old lady who wore an apron as grey as her hair, wheeled in a cart weighed down by plates of lemon-sugar crêpes and a carousel of tiny cakes, custard slices and a pyramid of profiteroles.

All of the boys turned their heads towards Monsieur Xavier as he poked a finger through each creamy, chocolate profiterole and inhaled them one by one.

"What a nerve he has! Eating like a king while we're left with scraps." Theo clenched his fists so hard that veins rose to the surface. "We deserve a feast of our own."

Bastien's chest swelled, inflating like a balloon. He admired Theo's fierce determination; it was contagious. "You're right. We'll be free of his chocolate-covered clutches one day."

Theo smiled. "One day might be sooner than you think."

"What do you mean?" Bastien heard the cogs whirring in Theo's brain.

"Patience, *mon ami*," Theo teased, a glint in his eye. "Let's just say, I've been working on something."

When something cold brushed against his foot that night, Bastien's first thought was that he was about to be eaten alive by a huge, black rat. The boys often spotted the creatures scurrying up the staircase in search of forgotten crumbs and warmer spots to hide. They nibbled on everything from blankets to Monsieur Xavier's supply of cheese wheels and now, it appeared, Bastien's feet. He kicked out in the darkness, fighting his furry, sharp-clawed opponent.

"*Aïe!*" His not-so-furry and definitely-not-sharp-clawed opponent jumped up from the foot of the bed. "That hurt."

"Theo!" Bastien hissed. "What are you doing?"

"We're going on an adventure." Theo pulled an object out of his back pocket.

Even in the darkness, Bastien could make out something glinting. It beckoned to him and he sat upright.

"Is that what I think it is?"

"*Mais oui!* The finest lockpick in the whole of Paris, made from Chef's hairpins. It's taken me ages to find ones thin enough to work." Theo laughed. "For someone who bathes in kitchen grease, Chef really does care an awful lot about her hair."

"Will it work?" Bastien studied the bent metal wires. They didn't look like the key to freedom.

"Have a little faith in me, would you? Your lack of belief is almost insulting."

"It's not you, it's Monsieur Xavier. What about him? He'll notice we've gone." Bastien couldn't hide the anxiety in his voice. It gave him away, like a magician with baggy sleeves.

"Don't worry about him. Do you really think he spends his evenings working away in his office? You're not the only one who stays up after bedtime."

Bastien paused. "What do you mean?"

"I've kept my eye on his comings and goings," Theo whispered. "He locks us in here at eight o'clock and doesn't check up on us again until midnight. I tested my lockpick two nights ago and he was nowhere to be found. Where he goes during that time, I don't know, but it gives us four hours."

Bastien hesitated. His worries were never more than a step behind; a big, grey cloud that seemed to follow him around since he'd arrived at the orphanage.

"*Allez!*" Theo urged. "How can you write about adventures if you don't have them? Everything we see is grey and duller than the water we wash in. Outside, the city is waiting for us!"

Bastien glanced around the dormitory. The other boys were sleeping soundly, the usual high-pitched snores coming from Fred and Felix. Robin rustled in his blanket and low-pitched melodies came from Sami's bed.

"We won't escape for good without the others," Theo added. "We're family. If this works, then I'll find a way for all of us to get out of here. Soon. But tonight, your imagination is in need of an adventure."

Bastien heard Paris call out his name and he longed to answer, but ever since he'd been sent to the orphanage, he'd felt abandoned by the world outside. What if he visited Le Chat Curieux and Alice wanted nothing to do with him?

Yet he couldn't deny how good it would feel to be in the city once again. The inspiration he needed to continue the story his parents had started lived outside these four walls. Theo was right. He needed to feel like himself again and if he was to write about adventures, he had to go on one of his own.

"*D'accord*. Let's go before I change my mind."

Bastien pulled on his trousers and buttoned his only jacket over his flannel nightshirt. Outside would be cold, but the thrill of what he was about to do would keep him warm all night. He slipped on his scuffed, black shoes and followed Theo.

It turned out that Theo could pick locks as well as Robin picked his nose, and within a minute they were out of the dormitory and tiptoeing across the hallway, heading for the staircase. With every noise – a floorboard creaking or the wind whistling – Bastien jumped out of his skin.

They took two steps at a time and reached the bottom of the staircase in seconds. Creeping across the hallway towards the entrance, they heard clanging pans and the tired sighs of Chef coming from behind the kitchen door.

"She's probably already preparing Monsieur Xavier's thirteen-course breakfast." Theo frowned.

The giant iron door of the orphanage entrance stood before them like a barricade.

"*Euh*," Theo said, tucking his hair behind his ears in concentration. "This one might take a bit longer."

Bastien watched as Theo threaded the metal stalk into the first lock, twisting and turning it about like a corkscrew. He muttered in frustration, but Bastien kept quiet. He knew that telling Theo to hurry up was pointless; just as Bastien could never rush the telling of a story, Theo couldn't rush an invention.

What felt like an hour had only been five minutes, but when the last lock made a satisfying click, Bastien almost shouted with delight.

They slipped out into the sharp night air. Theo had done it. They were outside.

"This way!" Theo led them through the courtyard, dodging bits of statues that had been broken during Monsieur Xavier's last rage. Through the wild weeds, they scaled the gates as quickly as the ivy that grew up the railings. Bastien's trouser leg caught on a spike and he tugged it free.

They jumped down, landing on the other side like cats, their movements delicate and precise. Bastien's eyes widened in amazement and Theo grinned back. They didn't need to say anything, for they both knew what the other was feeling: freedom.

Bastien breathed in the smell of the city as they walked through the cobbled streets, weaving in and out of the tiny alleyways that flowed like veins. But, walking past Luxembourg Gardens, their feet became too impatient.

"Last one to the river is a *fromage*-sniffer!" Bastien teased.

And they ran head first into the beating heart of the city.

RETURN TO LE CHAT CURIEUX

The excitement of seeing the city in all its night-time glory made Bastien's heart beat triple-time. That, or the fact that he'd just sprinted for the first time in his life. He'd never been one for exercise. At school, when it was time for their weekly ball games, Bastien always claimed a sore stomach and sought refuge in the library. He hid among the stacks, preferring to stretch the muscles in his brain than the ones in his legs.

They came to a stop near the river's edge and sat down on a bench to catch their breath. It was bitterly cold and the sky was heavy with the likelihood of snow, but Bastien felt nothing but freedom. On the left bank of the river, the sound of saxophones and butter-smooth jazz floated from the bars, where the night was only just starting for the men and women dressed in their finest evening wear. Across the water, the towers of Notre-Dame ruled the skyline, while the river's surface sparkled with lights from passing boats.

He'd forgotten just how beautiful Paris was; it was a city that offered you everything, even when you had nothing to give in return. Families passed by, walking along the Seine, wrapped in thick woollen coats and knitted scarves. Bastien wrapped his arms around his threadbare jacket. He wished his mother was here to sweep him into her long wool overcoat, which had always cocooned him in warmth. He swallowed down the sadness in his throat as he thought of the memories he'd made on these streets with his parents.

Tonight, he would make new ones with Theo.

"Where shall we go?" Bastien asked. If only for a few hours, the monotony of orphanage life was on pause. Monsieur Xavier, the terrible food, the endless chores, the Isolation Chamber. None of it existed out here.

"Your turn first." Theo smiled. "You decide."

Bastien knew right away. He'd dreamed of the same creaking bookshelves for months. He missed the dark, cosy corners and the constant smell of butter and pastry. But most of all, he missed Alice, Charlotte and Jules and he hoped, desperately so, that they had missed him too.

"Let's go to Le Chat Curieux."

Theo rolled his eyes. "You are entirely predictable." He got to his feet and bowed to Bastien. "Lead the way, then."

They took a left turn that led them deeper into the twisty streets. Bastien marvelled at the Saint-Michel fountain with its high arches and red marble columns. Stone dragons spurted water at the foot of the sculpted angel and, as they passed through the square, Bastien picked up a pebble and threw it into the water.

His last visit to the bookshop in the summer already felt like a lifetime ago, but he remembered the route as if it was stamped on the back of his hand. Bastien raced round the last corner and there it was: Le Chat Curieux, with its archway of books curved neatly around the emerald-green door and its sign, a spectacled black cat with its whiskers in a book, swaying gently in the night breeze.

They peered through the bookshop window and Bastien was surprised to find it still open and busy. People, dressed in smart suits and knee-length dresses, stood chatting and throwing their hands around in wild gestures. A large man with a thick black moustache sneezed and snot splattered onto the windowpane. The man frantically fished a handkerchief from his front pocket, while Bastien and Theo did their best not to collapse with laughter.

"Come on," Bastien said, between excited breaths. "Let's see what's going on." He opened the front door, the bell chiming their arrival.

Le Chat Curieux was still the same, yet tonight it looked magical and brand-new to Bastien. The labyrinth of ceiling-high bookshelves had no end and the walls were as colourful as he remembered, full of bright paintings and posters. Bastien hoped his favourite reading spot was still at the back of the shop: an old moss-green chaise longue hidden behind thick, velvet curtains. It was a reading room all of one's own and he recalled many afternoons there sitting alongside Alice, their noses buried in books and comics.

The only thing that looked different to Bastien were the people in the bookshop. They were gathered in groups, talking in hushed tones and taking small sips from their drinks. No one was browsing the shelves. Everyone looked worried. What exactly was going on tonight?

"Argh!" Theo yelled, tripping over in fright. Something furry had wrapped itself around his legs. It was Babette, the bookshop cat.

"I think she likes you." Bastien bent down to stroke Babette, laughing as Theo tried to wrestle his trouser leg out of her paws. He scanned the room as he stood, trying to spot his most favourite, familiar face. Where was Alice? She had to be here somewhere, and hopefully, happy to see him too.

"Bastien!" The piercing call of his name stopped everyone in their tracks. He looked up and there she was; Alice bundled down the stairs, her green-patterned skirt billowing around her like a parachute. She parted the crowd with her flapping arms and flung herself at him.

"I thought I'd never see you again," she whispered. Alice's hug erased all of the worries he'd had about their friendship, like chalk being wiped from a blackboard. When she finally let go, after untangling her long, honeycomb hair from Bastien's jacket buttons, he introduced her to Theo, who bowed awkwardly.

"I've been so worried about you. I wrote letters until my hand ached, but you never replied." Alice's voice wobbled and she squeezed his hand as though she couldn't quite believe he was actually there. "I thought

49

something terrible had happened to you. I tried to see you at the orphanage but some wicked man wouldn't let me past the gates. He said my name wasn't on the visitor list!"

Her words tore Bastien's heart apart and pieced it back together again. He felt a pang of guilt for thinking that Alice would ever abandon him. Of course she'd sent him letters and tried to visit. Monsieur Xavier had been deliberately blocking all communication to the orphanage! Still he couldn't bring himself to tell Alice the truth straight away – that something terrible *had* happened to him; that he was under the watch of an awful man who spent every waking moment making his life a misery.

Because Bastien didn't want Alice's pity. Right here in the bookshop, he felt somewhere almost close to normal. He wanted to hold onto that feeling a while longer. It had been a long time since he'd felt that way.

"I'm sorry I haven't received any of your letters. They might've got lost in the post. The orphanage is fine, the director is just strict." Bastien looked at Theo, willing him to agree.

"That's right." Theo coughed.

Alice looked at Bastien, plainly unconvinced. "Fine?

It looked like it was falling apart!"

"I'm fine. *Je te promets*. It's just an old building."

"Well, I'm so glad you're here. Both of you." Alice's face relaxed slightly, although Bastien could tell she didn't quite believe him yet. "Tonight hasn't exactly been much fun."

"What's going on?" Bastien asked as she led them to the back of the bookshop. They weaved through the crowd; people swarmed around each other, passing plates of tiny canapés back and forth like worker bees. Theo swiped a handful of cheese-and-mushroom tarts and passed one to Bastien. The sweet cheese melted in his mouth instantly.

Alice parted the velvet curtains and beckoned them to follow. Bastien felt a calm wash over him as they crammed onto the end of the chaise longue. His favourite spot in the bookshop hadn't changed.

"My parents were meant to be hosting a party tonight for their friend, Gaston LeGrand," Alice said. "His new publishing company is doing very well. They're calling him the future of books."

A memory floated to the surface at the mention of LeGrand's name. Bastien remembered his parents talking about the very same man the night before they'd left for Cannes. LeGrand had wanted to publish their next book. Bastien wished he knew what they'd been planning to write. He thought about how his father had seemed worried that evening. Had he been nervous about whether their next story was good enough?

"But the mood has taken a turn for the worse," Alice continued, pulling Bastien back to the conversation. "Delphine de la Reine went missing a couple of nights ago. She's a writer, one of Maman's friends. They wanted to cancel the whole thing but LeGrand insisted everyone still came to work out how to find her. Maman is certain she was kidnapped."

"How awful!" Bastien's skin turned cold.

"Why is your mother so certain she was kidnapped?" Theo asked. "What if she ran away?"

Alice shook her head. "Delphine wouldn't do that. She has two small children who she adores. Besides, she isn't the only writer who's gone missing recently. She's the fourth in the last two months."

"*Quoi?*" Theo almost choked on his last tart crust.

"How do you know all of this?" Bastien asked.

"It's in every newspaper all over France," Alice said. "They don't have a firm suspect yet but a witness described a tall, dark-haired man wearing a red-lined cloak acting suspiciously outside a Métro stop. That last bit isn't in the news though, I overheard Maman talking to someone tonight." Alice looked down guiltily. "Eavesdropping is sometimes necessary."

While she chatted with Theo about eavesdropping inventions, Bastien replayed Alice's revelation in his mind. Writers were vanishing in Paris, snatched out of thin air by a possible kidnapper. Why was this happening? And who would do such a thing? He thought of families missing their loved ones and all of the questions swimming around in their minds. He thought of children without their parents and the sting of not knowing what had happened to the people who were meant to protect you.

Bastien had questions too, about how his parents had been taken away from him. He pinched the inside of his finger to keep his tears behind his eyes.

Alice noticed the look on Bastien's face. "Why don't we go and find my parents?" She jumped to her feet. "They'll be thrilled to see you. Maman is probably in the kitchen, making more cakes. She always says sugar is the best remedy for worry."

"Yes, let's go and find some more of those tarts," Theo said. "They're the best thing I've eaten in months!"

Bastien closed the velvet curtains behind him and followed Alice and Theo back across the bookshop, but his mind was elsewhere. He saw the concern on the faces of those here tonight. Bastien had locked his own concern away in a corner of his mind, when the police had swept him away to the orphanage. Ever since then he'd simply been trying to make it through the months without incurring Monsieur Xavier's wrath, but had he been too focused on surviving when he should've been remembering? Amongst the sea of worried faces in the bookshop, Bastien felt his own fears about his parents' fate resurfacing like flotsam.

"Maman," Alice called. "Look who's here!"

Bastien tore his gaze away from the anxious guests, and spotted Charlotte balancing a tray of lemon cakes.

Charlotte turned around, her hair unravelling around her flour-dusted face from its once-neat bun. She spotted Bastien and squealed, dropping her tray. Cakes bounced all over the bookshop floor as she rushed towards him. Theo darted towards the newly-liberated cakes, scooping them up into his arms.

"What a sight for sore eyes!" Charlotte's hug swept over Bastien like a wave. Breathing in the rich smell of buttery pastry on her apron, he felt his mind relax slightly. Her voice was as sweet as brioche; everything about Charlotte was sweet, from her golden-blonde hair to her fondant-flavoured personality. She was head baker of the bookshop café and her treats had people visiting from the city and beyond, to fill their stomachs as well as their bookshelves. No visit was complete without the taste of a warm croissant with home-made jam and hot chocolate so thick it could only be eaten with a spoon.

"Look how you've already grown!" She shook her head in disbelief and Bastien spotted the concerned look she cast over his torn trousers. "We've tried to visit every month but that fool of a director said it was against the rules." She paused for breath. "He said only family members are on the visitor list, which is frankly ridiculous."

"Calm down, Maman. At least we've got Bastien back for tonight." Alice beamed.

Charlotte dusted off her apron. "Well, I've written a letter of complaint to the district's town hall. They ought to be running such a place properly. If they don't reply within the week, I'll be paying them a visit."

Bastien smiled. "*Merci.*" He was grateful for Charlotte's efforts, but he suspected that any letter detailing Monsieur Xavier's shortcomings would almost certainly disappear without a trace.

"Ah, but how good it is to see you. You are still just as handsome as your father." Charlotte pinched his cheeks.

"Stop! You're embarrassing him," Alice moaned. "Anyway, where's that father of mine?"

"Putting up more posters, *mon ange*," Charlotte replied softly.

"Come on, you two! Let's go and say hello." Alice grabbed Theo's free hand and pulled him into the crowd. The look on his face made Bastien laugh; he'd never seen Theo look so excited.

Just as Bastien smiled at Charlotte and made to join his friends, something eclipsed his view inside the bookshop. A tall shadow fell over him and as he turned around, Bastien found himself face to face with a skyscraper of a man.

"*Excusez-moi.*" The man's voice was deep and booming, like a loudspeaker.

"It's my fault. I wasn't looking where I was going," Bastien said hurriedly, his eyes flickering over the man in front of him. Where had Alice and Theo gone? He couldn't see them anywhere.

"It's quite alright." The man turned to Charlotte. "I absolutely must have another one of your cakes. Are there any left?"

Charlotte smiled awkwardly. "I'm afraid I dropped my last batch. Oh, where are my manners? This is Bastien, Margot and Hugo's son. Bastien, meet Gaston LeGrand."

At the mention of his parents, Bastien's attention

changed direction. Now he looked properly at LeGrand. The man wore a sharp grey suit, complete with a blue bow tie and a large trilby hat.

"I was terribly sorry to hear about your parents. They were great writers and kind souls too." LeGrand's face changed as he spoke. It had been straight and full of hard lines, but talking about his parents, Bastien noticed how it turned soft at the edges.

"They were." Bastien swallowed the lump in his throat, thinking of all the stories that had disappeared along with his parents. LeGrand's kind words made him feel brave and he told himself to act upon this feeling. It didn't always last very long.

"I write too."

"What was that?" LeGrand bent down.

"I'm a writer too," Bastien said, louder. Words leaped from the tip of his tongue. "I have been, ever since I was old enough to hold a pen. I'm writing a story at the moment, actually. Would you like to read it?" he stuttered. "I mean, once it's finished."

"What's it about?" LeGrand asked while Charlotte quietly excused herself.

"I'm not sure yet. I plan to finish the story my parents started."

A pause lingered, long enough to make Bastien squirm awkwardly. Then LeGrand's face lit up like a neon sign.

"I'd love to read your story once it is finished. I am looking for new work to purchase and I'm certain that the son of Margot and Hugo Bonlivre is destined to become a great storyteller."

Bastien stayed calm and collected, but his insides exploded like fireworks on Bastille Day. If he could complete his story, it could have the potential to change his future. If LeGrand bought it then maybe Bastien could buy a house all of his own, with the other boys, and take Chef with them as their guardian too? They wouldn't have to wait until they were eighteen. He could create a new home for all of them, one without Monsieur Xavier.

Ever since the summer Bastien had felt as though nothing good would ever happen to him again without his parents, and that life would be as flat as the beaches of Normandy. Now his stomach bubbled with the possibility of a new type of dream: to write a story worth sharing with the world and to follow in his parents' footsteps.

"*Merci*." Bastien beamed. "This means everything to me."

LeGrand tipped his hat. "You and your story can find me here at the bookshop. I come every Saturday morning."

"I'll write it as quickly as my fingers can manage."

"There's no rush, dear boy." LeGrand's face crinkled and he rested his hand on Bastien's shoulder. "*À bientôt*, Bastien. I look forward to reading your story. In these trying times, we need new, hopeful stories more than ever."

Standing still was impossible. As soon as LeGrand disappeared from view, Bastien raced over to the window where he'd spotted Theo and Alice juggling stacks of posters. Jules stood next to them, his half-moon glasses slipping down his nose.

"So the rumours are true." Jules greeted him with a strong, bear-like hug, his tall frame making Bastien feel as small as an ant. "It's brilliant to see you again."

Bastien took a poster from him. The picture was of Delphine de la Reine, wearing a toothy smile on her face and a spotted scarf around her neck. The text underneath said she'd last been seen leaving the theatre near the Saint-Lazare station just after ten o'clock, but had never arrived at her Métro stop.

Something strange was happening in Paris. People didn't just vanish into thin air.

A thought resurfaced. It had always been there, hovering at the edges of Bastien's mind, but tonight the bookshop had given him clearer headspace than the orphanage could ever offer.

Hotels didn't just mysteriously set alight, either.

He and every other person in France knew the same tragic tale, of an unexpected hotel fire, but what if it had been no accident? What if it had been planned? Like the possible kidnapper lurking outside the Métro station for Delphine, had someone been outside his parents' hotel room, waiting to start a fire?

Bastien thought back to the newspaper coverage of his parents' death. His only sources of information in the orphanage were the papers that Chef read every morning and left on the kitchen countertops. While he'd been chopping onions for dinner one evening, Bastien had come across an article with an update about the police enquiry. They had interviewed every guest in the hotel – all except one. The man staying in the room opposite had checked out in the early hours of the morning and never been traced. Regardless, the results of their investigation led the police to believe the fire had been accidental.

Still, knowing and believing something to be true

were two different things.

Who was the man the police had never been able to find? A monumental question struck Bastien. Could it be the same man involved with Delphine's disappearance? If he was targeting writers, then had he started with Bastien's parents? What if the man who had kidnapped Delphine had tried to kidnap his parents too, but something had gone terribly wrong?

Bastien's grip loosened and the poster fluttered to the floor. His palms were laced with sweat, his mind racing with the connections it was trying to make. Was his imagination getting the better of him? Or was there something there, just waiting to be pieced together?

"Everything okay?" Theo looked down at the poster then back at Bastien. "Do you feel unwell?"

Bastien managed a half-smile. He couldn't yet voice his thoughts out loud, for when he did they would become real. And he knew all too well how impossible it was to ignore reality.

The next hour flew by full of conversation, which Bastien was grateful for. He needed a distraction from the battle raging in his head. He chatted with an American man, who'd driven ambulances in the war and was now living in Paris to write his own book, and a woman called Paulette who'd not long left her home country of Martinique to come and study at the Sorbonne. When Theo nudged him in the ribs, Bastien looked up at the grandfather clock reluctantly. It was eleven o'clock. They had to be back before Monsieur Xavier's midnight inspection.

At the door, while saying their goodbyes, Charlotte handed Bastien and Theo a chocolate croissant each. Jules was wiping dust from a tall stack of books behind the door and Bastien glanced at the top of the pile. *The King's Return* by Olivier Odieux looked as old as Jules, maybe even older.

"Olivier Odieux writes books faster than we can sell them." Jules looked at the book like it was one of Babette's bad smells. "I'm not a fan, though. He's made a fortune telling the same story over and over, in different disguises."

"We'll find a way to come and see you," Alice interrupted, flinging herself at Bastien again. "I'll carry on writing to you, but if you don't get my letters and I have to scale the gates, then so be it." They hugged tightly; he really didn't want to let go of her. He wanted to stay right here with everyone in the bookshop. What he'd found out about Delphine and the other missing writers clung to his every thought like a spider to its web. If there was a possibility that it was all connected to what had happened to his parents in Cannes, then he would chase down the truth until his legs buckled beneath him.

"I think," Theo mused, as they closed the bookshop door behind them and he bit into his pastry, "that I'm in love with this croissant." Chocolate ganache oozed from its middle and he licked his fingers clean. "That's entirely normal, isn't it?"

Croissants eaten, Bastien and Theo ran back through the city as quickly as their feet would carry them. When the crooked roof of the orphanage came into view, the dread that had disappeared for a little while at the bookshop returned to invade Bastien's mind like an army of bad thoughts.

"You're worried about Delphine de la Reine, aren't you?" Theo said, as they crept across the courtyard. An owl hooted at them from its perch on a broken flowerpot. "You acted strange after Alice mentioned she'd gone missing."

"It's more than that." Bastien paused. He could confide in Theo. "What Alice said made me think of my parents. About whether what happened to them was actually an accident. There was a dark-haired man there that night too, near their hotel room. The police were never able to find him during their enquiries."

Theo frowned. "You think someone, maybe this man, started the fire on purpose?" His voice dropped as he fiddled with the main door lock. He tucked his long, curly brown hair behind his ears, but it fell forward again.

"I know it's strange, but it doesn't feel like a coincidence." Bastien's voice cracked with emotion. "What if this man tried to kidnap my parents but ended up doing something far worse?"

"Wait a minute! What are you saying?" Theo turned to Bastien, his eyes wide in understanding. "You think the same man who kidnapped Delphine started the hotel fire?"

"Maybe." Bastien knew it was a stretch of the imagination, but Theo hadn't looked at him like he was talking nonsense. If his friend believed him, then he would believe in himself too. "If he's targeting writers, it makes sense. You heard what Alice said, about all the other writers who've gone missing."

"But the kidnappings have only happened recently,"

Theo said between exasperated grunts as the lockpick jammed in the lock.

"After what happened to my parents, perhaps it stopped for a while? Maybe the man didn't want to get caught." Bastien's jaw wobbled. "Something might not have gone to plan that night at the hotel."

The door unlocked with a click and the two of them hurried across the threshold. "I'm going to follow this feeling and find out the truth," Bastien continued. "Whatever it takes."

"Count me in." Theo placed a hand on Bastien's shoulder. "We'll find out together, *whatever it takes*."

After Theo relocked the door, they crept up the stairs and walked on tiptoes back through the dormitory.

As soon as Bastien's head hit his pillow, he fell asleep. Maybe it was because of his full stomach or maybe it was because his head and heart were exhausted from the unanswered mysteries of Delphine's disappearance, his parents and the hotel fire.

THE WRETCHED OLIVIER ODIEUX

On the other side of Paris, Olivier Odieux sat in his attic study at the top of his grand house perched on the highest hill of Montmartre. From his window, he stared out at the twinkling lights of the Eiffel Tower in the distance as they painted the bare canvas of the black night sky. People would've killed for such a view. Olivier had. But tonight, the city lights were mocking him, so he closed the shutters and turned away.

He was a page into his latest book, a tale of a young prince claiming his right to the throne. It was the first time in fifteen years that Olivier was trying to write a book completely by himself. Such desperate measures were needed. He'd got rid of one problem over the summer, but another had presented itself and then everything had started to spiral out of control like an automobile with no driver. He was worried.

Olivier was an awful man and a doubly awful writer, who had long made his living off stolen ideas. When he was younger, Olivier had written a book that was adored throughout France. Unfortunately, no new ideas ever came to him after that, and so he'd started to collect other people's ideas like a museum curator. His entire career was based on the only skills he possessed, which were, arguably, not skills to be proud of: cheating and stealing.

Olivier produced twenty books a year and when journalists asked him about the secret to his writing success, he would merely wink and say, "If I told you, I'd have to kill you." The journalists laughed and Olivier let them. It was better for them to think he was joking when, in fact, he would easily have pushed each of them off the Arc de Triomphe while thinking about what he was going to have for dinner.

His secret was money. Lots of it, left to him by his family. He filled the bank accounts of other writers, and in return they pledged their ideas, and their silence. His team of writers had served him well, but then fame had turned him blind with greed and now the family fortune was almost completely gone. When the writers had discovered Olivier had spent the money he owed them on a new yacht, they'd ripped up their work and left him with five books to write in just six weeks.

There was a nervous knock on the door and a small, smartly-dressed timid-looking man hovered at the threshold. Louis Odieux was only five years older than Olivier, yet the stress of cleaning up his brother's messes had aged him considerably. Now he was as bald as an egg, apart from the pencil moustache that clung to his top lip.

Once upon a time, Louis had greatly enjoyed the success that surrounded him thanks to his brother's fame. They'd sailed the Riviera and foolishly gambled away thousands of francs in Monaco casinos. But as the years had passed, and Olivier's desperation to stay in the spotlight worsened, Louis felt increasingly uneasy. Now, with five books to complete by Christmas and a near-empty bank account, Louis worried all the good times they'd had would soon end.

"What is it?" Olivier barked, turning so violently in his chair that his neck looked close to snapping. His mouth was curled in a permanent snarl. The few thin strands of his hair that remained clung to the side of his head like overcooked spaghetti, and the wrinkles running across his forehead were as deep as the potholes on the Rue de Rivoli.

"Your editors just called." Louis's voice quivered, as did the hairs on his moustache. He was always nervous when he spoke to Olivier, but lately holding a conversation with him was like daring to play poker with a bad hand. His moods had become even more unpredictable.

"They wanted to remind you that there's only six weeks left until the deadline. Is there any—"

Olivier roared, throwing his heavy typewriter onto the floor with alarming ease. It shattered into a hundred pieces.

"I know when the deadline is! And I'd be able to work much quicker without your constant interruptions."

"You're quite right." Louis took a cautious step backwards, shielding himself behind a large potted plant. He unbuttoned his top button and pulled at his collar, which suddenly felt like it was trying to choke him.

"I'm not happy about writing them myself. This new plan of ours has got off to a bumpy start." Olivier slouched back in his chair, his teeth grinding as he spoke.

"Delphine de la Reine wouldn't know a good ending if it wrote itself."

"I'll let Xavier know," Louis replied. "I'll tell him to prioritize older writers with more experience next time."

Olivier kicked the crumpled balls of typewriter paper around the room. "Speaking of Xavier, what news from our *petit frère*?"

Louis winced as Olivier's voice mellowed at the mention of their youngest brother. Xavier Odieux made so many mistakes but Olivier had an obvious soft spot for him, and it had turned Louis as bitter as coffee. Olivier had long favoured Xavier, always entrusting him with the most important of tasks. There were many secrets between the two of them and Louis knew there were meetings he wasn't invited to and conversations he wasn't a part of. His brothers had always undervalued Louis. Everyone usually did.

"He called earlier. It would appear that there's still no trace of the notebook."

Olivier's face flashed with crimson panic. He had a short temper and often flew off the handle, but this was something different. Louis had never seen his brother look so worried. The notebook had him rattled.

"Don't worry, I'll arrange a meeting with Xavier." Louis hoped his firm words would calm Olivier.

"Don't tell *me* not to worry!" Olivier sank back into his desk chair. "That notebook is the biggest thorn in my side. What the Bonlivres knew is too dangerous to be out there, out of my control. It could ruin everything. I *have* to get my hands on it."

Louis fiddled with his shirtsleeves. "And what exactly did they know? Perhaps if I knew, I could help—"

"*Ça suffit!*" Olivier shot down the question. "Fetch me a new typewriter and make yourself scarce." He dismissed Louis with a careless flick of the wrist.

Louis bowed and tiptoed out of the room, closing the door gently behind him. It was only when he was at the bottom of the attic staircase that he let out a great breath, one full of despair and disappointment. For so long, he'd honoured his parents' wish to take care of Olivier and Xavier. Family looked after family, but Louis had lost himself in the storm that was his brothers and he could no longer see clearly. He fiddled with the gold chain around his neck; it had been a present from Philippe, his partner who he had loved so deeply, and it always gave him an extra dash of courage.

One day, Louis told himself, he would find the strength to walk away and go back to his old life, perhaps with Philippe if he could forgive Louis for abandoning him to blindly follow his brothers. One day, he would be done with the Odieux name for good.

But today was not that day.

The hours after midnight always spelled mischief, and Monsieur Xavier was no stranger to creating some of his own. As night seeped into morning, he tiptoed down the orphanage stairs and headed for the entrance. He drew his keys from his top cloak pocket and unlocked the various bolts and chains. Slipping out into the courtyard, he pulled his hood up to conceal his face. The night called to him. He hated spending his days in this place surrounded by such ungrateful children. Why hadn't Olivier asked Louis to run the orphanage instead? Their oldest brother was useless and Xavier couldn't help but feel his own talents were being wasted.

With the boys all accounted for and securely locked in, he was left with hours to complete his next task. He never liked to rush a kidnapping anyway, it unsettled him. Kidnappings were best carried out as though making a perfect cup of tea; the longer the brew time, the better the result.

Monsieur Xavier knew that the famous author Jacques Joli worked till the early hours in a dingy café a few steps away from the Place de la Concorde. Far from being a popular place to sip on hot drinks, the all-night café was run by a grumpy man who overcharged customers and underpaid staff, so much so that the last waiter had finally quit last week.

Which made it the perfect place to write in peace.

And the perfect place to kidnap a writer.

If anything had the ability to break the boring routine of orphanage life, it was the weekly school class. The other boys had told Bastien tales of their exciting, daily lessons when Monsieur Dupont had been in charge. They'd learned about fizzing chemical reactions, performed plays and read classic books, went cross-country running in the city parks and made desserts of all kinds in the kitchen with Chef. The time that Felix had eaten ten helpings of crème brûlée in one go was a legendary tale amongst the boys.

But in Monsieur Xavier's very important and not at all humble opinion, learning was a privilege that the boys weren't entitled to seven days a week and so the daily classes had become just one. Now, every Friday, the boys rose from their beds, unsure of what they would learn.

"*Vite!* Quickly, get to class." Monsieur Xavier pulled the blanket from Robin's bed. Robin wore thick-rimmed glasses which had broken a long time ago and cracks now crept across the lenses. The poor boy could never see the director coming.

"You should consider yourself lucky to have me as your teacher." Monsieur Xavier bared his coffee-stained teeth in a humourless grin. Robin tried to pull the blanket back over his head to avoid the brown flecks of spit that flew out of Monsieur Xavier's mouth as he spoke. "You're all in desperate need of a proper education."

The boys marched down the staircase and into the dining hall, where the wooden benches had been pushed to one side and a tall blackboard on wheels stood in the middle of the room.

"Take your seats," Monsieur Xavier barked. He twirled a piece of chalk in his hand as though it was a weapon, and stood in front of the blackboard.

"What do you think he'll teach us today?" Bastien whispered to Theo. "Maybe the importance of dental hygiene?"

"Bastien Bonlivre!" Monsieur Xavier's voice cut through the hall. "If you dare speak another word you'll be on the menu for dinner tonight."

Bastien's eyes dropped to the floor. He didn't dare look up again until Monsieur Xavier turned his back to write on the blackboard.

"If Chef turned you into a pie, would you judge me for eating you?" Theo said, his shoulders shaking with laughter.

Bastien stifled a snort. "If she served me warm with a side of potatoes, I'd eat me too."

"Silence!" Monsieur Xavier screeched, turning around as quick as a flash. His eyes bore into Bastien's like a hot poker. "If you think you know everything, then why don't you come up and teach the class today?"

"*Desolé*, Monsieur Xavier."

"You think that you're more intelligent than me, don't you?"

Bastien shook his head. He didn't want to anger the man further. "No, not at all. I'm only twelve."

Monsieur Xavier threw the piece of chalk at the wall behind the boys. They all ducked instinctively.

"Yes, that's right. You're a child and I'm an adult. I hold the answers to all the questions about your sad little lives. Now be quiet and get your exercise books out. Today I'll be covering the art of war. We'll start with the importance of spying on your enemies."

Timothée, who declared at any given opportunity that he was a lover not a fighter, frowned. The others looked at each other helplessly. Monsieur Xavier's curriculum was far from ordinary. So far in classes he'd lectured them on how to create the perfect camouflage – which admittedly Theo had been quite interested in – how to make fake banknotes, and the importance of "traditional" values, whatever that meant.

Bastien's concentration drifted as he scribbled in his exercise book. The memories of last night, in the bookshop, played like a film in his mind, but the orphanage had a way of casting its grey veil over any happiness. Bastien knew it wouldn't be long before his golden memories of seeing Alice again and meeting LeGrand faded. Why was he here in the care of a crooked man, when he should be with his friends, searching for answers about the missing writers and his parents?

Just when the boys thought the day couldn't get any worse, Monsieur Xavier marched them straight back up to the dormitory before dinnertime and sent them to their beds. Theo glanced at Bastien, a confused look on his face. They knew Monsieur Xavier's routine like clockwork. This wasn't normal.

Bastien's stomach rumbled as loud as a Métro train rattling at full speed. He tried to ignore his hunger but smells of cooked chicken and strong cheeses wafted through the air. He couldn't be sure whether it was Chef preparing Monsieur Xavier's dinner or if he was simply imagining it.

"Because of Bastien's undesirable behaviour in class, this will be your dinner tonight." Monsieur Xavier walked up and down the rows of beds, throwing stale baguette ends at each boy.

Bastien squirmed deeper under his blanket, wishing it possessed the magical ability to transport him to a distant land. The further away from Monsieur Xavier, the better. The director singled him out each time and now, because of him, the others would go hungry.

"From now on, you will receive two hot meals a day. Three is a luxury you no longer deserve."

The boys fumed but did their best to not show the despair on their faces. Two meals were better than one, or none.

Monsieur Xavier shot the boys one final, trademark withering look and slammed the door behind him, the locks clicking into place.

Silence hung over the dormitory like a curtain call. Bastien wished he could magic all of them out of there. He so desperately wished that Charlotte's complaint to the town hall would be enough to get Monsieur Xavier fired. Next time he saw Alice, he would no longer spare her the truth. He would tell her just how bad it was here. Perhaps a kinder director, just like Monsieur Dupont, would come and take care of the boys until they were of age. Or perhaps Bastien and Theo needed to start thinking about a proper escape plan. With Theo's lockpick, all of them could be free. But where would they go? They'd need money to take care of themselves and Bastien's story for LeGrand was still nothing more than pages of crossed-out scribbles.

A sob rippled around the room, breaking the silence. Robin was the youngest boy and cried most nights, ever since Monsieur Xavier had put bars on the only window. The others had done everything to try to console him: Timothée had put on a puppet show and Theo had even made him a rag doll from Chef's drying cloths, but each night Robin left the patchwork doll at the end of his bed, unwanted and unloved. Just like he felt.

As Bastien sat in bed, an idea knocked on his brain. It came fast and fully formed and it made his stomach flip like a crêpe in a frying pan. Since last night, all he'd been able to think about was the strange circumstances of the missing writers and whether they were connected to his parents. It was exhausting. If a story could distract him from his own thoughts and his rumbling stomach too, then maybe it would do the same for the other boys.

"Who wants to hear a story?"

The patter of feet filled the room and within seconds all the boys had gathered at the foot of Bastien's bed. All except Sami, who grunted and rolled onto his side. He probably considered himself too old for tales, but Bastien knew it was physically impossible to grow out of stories.

Bastien looked at Robin sitting eagerly, clutching his knees. His eyes were still puffy and wet behind his glasses, but they were big and bright; a curiosity of blue. It was exactly the inspiration Bastien needed.

"Let's begin.

"*There was once a young boy called Robin, who had never known what it was like to see clearly. On the day he was born,* the doctor had told his parents that over time it would become more difficult for their son to see the world.

"But watching the world was what Robin loved best. Every night, he'd sit at his bedroom window and look up at the night sky, watching the magic of the silvery lunar crescent and tracing the twinkling constellations with his fingertips.

"To see the sky clearly, he wore thick-rimmed glasses with lenses that magnified his eyes like a bug under a microscope. Other children would tease him, and each lunchtime the biggest bully would steal his glasses and pass them around the class, until they'd return to Robin, dirty and damaged.

"One Friday, on his way home from a particularly bad day at school, Robin bumped into a man on a street corner. He'd been so consumed by his own worries that he hadn't noticed him. Robin mumbled an apology, but the man waved it away. He'd been waiting for this boy for a long time.

"The man held out a small, brown box. If he'd been paying closer attention, Robin would have realized that the man had the sky in his eyes; instead of pupils, he had two white stars.

"'Take this,' the man said.

"Normally, he would never talk to strangers and certainly never accept gifts from them, but Robin felt sad and stuck, like he was trapped at the bottom of a dark well with no rope to pull himself up with.

"'Please,' the man insisted. He stretched out his hand, and Robin could no longer ignore his curiosity. Carefully, he took the brown leather box and opened it. It smelled warm and rich and inside was a gift even more beautiful: a pair of glasses made from pure gold with white lenses.

"'Put these on and you'll see the world clearer than ever,' the man instructed. 'Use them to create the world you want to see.'

"Robin wanted to ask the man what he meant, but when he looked up, the stranger was gone.

"That night, when Robin put the glasses on, he saw more of the world than he ever had before. He saw through buildings and walls and, most importantly, he saw through people. While someone bad might have used the glasses for unspeakable things, Robin knew that kindness was his superpower.

"The next day at school, his new glasses didn't go unnoticed and he saw the bully walking towards him across the playground. He told himself to be brave, for no harm could come to him now. As the bully came closer, Robin could see sadness seeping out of the boy's heart. He'd never noticed it before, how the bully's heart was punctured like a tyre. The bully tried to pull the glasses from Robin's face, but they didn't move. The glasses belonged to Robin and they'd never belong to anyone else.

"He looked up at the bully and smiled; it was one of those smiles that could charm enemies.

"'These glasses won't heal the hole in your heart,' Robin said gently.

"The bully stumbled back, confused by Robin's kindness. He took another step back and then another, until he fled from the playground.

"From that day on, the bully never bothered Robin ever again. In fact, he stopped being a bully altogether. Robin was one step closer to creating the world he wanted to see: a kinder one.

"The next time Robin opened his window to gaze up at the sky, two shooting stars flashed across the sky. And he was sure they'd winked right at him."

It was only when the story ended that Bastien properly looked at the sea of faces staring back at him. Robin clapped his hands in glee and flung himself at Bastien.

"I've never had a story about me before," he whispered.

"Everyone deserves their own story." Bastien smiled glumly. "I'm sorry you didn't get a proper dinner tonight."

Robin shrugged. "It's not your fault. We all see the

way Monsieur Xavier treats you. We may be young, but we all have brains." Robin hugged him one more time before trudging back to his bed. "Be careful."

As usual, Bastien was the last one to fall asleep. He scribbled in his notebook, ideas buzzing around his brain like a wasp near an ice cream on a summer's day. Just like Robin's story, Bastien needed to look at things differently. There was so much happening that he needed to piece together.

Could it really be possible that Delphine's disappearance and those of the other writers were connected to his parents? Was the tall, dark-haired man with the red cloak the same man who'd been staying in the hotel room opposite his parents? The one the police had never found? It wasn't the story his parents had probably imagined he'd tell, but this was his life now. This was the story he had to write, not just for himself but for LeGrand too. Bastien was certain all of the strands were connected; he just needed to figure out where they led.

Sleep finally called just before midnight. Bastien placed his notebook underneath his bed, slipping it under the loose floorboard. He pulled his blanket right up to his shoulders.

Across the room, he spotted Robin, fast asleep with a smile on his face. Bastien remembered his father telling him how a story was the only thing in the world that could detach the mind from the body. Tonight, the boys hadn't been inside the orphanage. They'd been in a brighter, better place: inside a story.

But Bastien knew that they deserved to escape for more than just one evening.

They all deserved to be free of Monsieur Xavier's rule.

8

MESSAGE ON A TYPEWRITER

It wasn't an honour to be given a special job by Monsieur Xavier. The word "special" meant something different at the orphanage. It didn't mean something good or better. "Special" wasn't helping Chef prepare a cake and sneaking a spoonful of leftover melted chocolate, nor was it being sent into the city on an errand and taking the long way back through the Tuileries Garden.

So when Monsieur Xavier grabbed Theo after breakfast and told him, very loudly, that he had a special job for him, panic was a natural reflex. Bastien could do nothing but watch and worry as his friend was marched away. Only that morning, Theo had whispered to

Bastien that he had a surprise in store tonight. Whatever the surprise was, Bastien hoped that Theo would be back in time for it.

Monsieur Xavier led Theo down the cellar stairs and, with each step, Theo grew sure that he was being led towards danger. The boys had conjured up ideas about what was lurking down there. The popular vote was a stash of gold that Monsieur Xavier had stolen from the vaults of the Bank of France. But much to Theo's disappointment, the cellar wasn't hiding a stolen fortune. It was just a room filled with crates and wooden barrels. Dust, as thick as a slice of cake, covered every surface. No one had been down here for a very long time.

At the end of the room was a door with two metal bolts at the top. Theo followed closely behind the director, and heard the clunking of keys in his pocket. His gut instinct was to turn and run, for the sound of keys always meant being locked away.

Monsieur Xavier opened the door and pushed Theo through into a room with a wooden workbench and a small stool tucked under it. In the middle loomed a monstrous mountain of twisted metal parts, glimmering from the fraction of light streaming in from a window the size of a dinner plate.

"What is this?" Theo asked, bemused and a little bit scared.

"I thought you were one of the clever ones, Theo," Monsieur Xavier replied. "These are typewriters that need to be fixed."

"Why are there so many?"

"If you know what's good for you, you'll keep your mouth shut before you choke on all those questions." Monsieur Xavier's eyes pierced through Theo's skin like a bullet. "You'll be let out once you've fixed them all," he continued, pointing an overgrown fingernail towards the pile of mangled metal. With a smirk, he closed the door and slid the bolts back into place.

Theo rolled up his sleeves and pushed the hair from his eyes. He'd long given up trying to tame his hair; the last time he'd run a brush through it, the handle had snapped clean in half. He picked his way through the pile of broken machines, and counted at least twenty typewriters. What were they doing here? He'd never seen any in the orphanage, not even in Monsieur Xavier's office during his one unfortunate visit there.

He pulled one battered typewriter from the pile. Its keys were broken and the ribbon spool needed replacing. It was a relatively easy fix with the tools he'd been left and he wondered if Monsieur Xavier would spot a missing screwdriver; one would come in handy to fix the many broken items around the orphanage.

Turning the typewriter in his hands, Theo noticed a mark scratched into the back. He held it up to the window, and slowly the mark turned into words.

Aidez-nous!

A shiver of suspicion ran up Theo's back. Who had been using this typewriter and why were they asking for help? He dropped the typewriter and it crashed against the stone floor. Where had they all come from? It didn't make any sense. He had to get out of here and tell Bastien what he'd seen, but there was no way that Monsieur Xavier would let him go just yet. Even with his lockpick in his pocket, he couldn't open the cellar door from the inside. The only way out was to fix this mangled heap of metal. Theo had to concentrate.

He thought about his parents and how he could never distract them while they were in the throes of a project. He'd watch them in their workshop until they took off their goggles, downed their tools and took Theo to their local pâtisserie in Les Halles. They'd eat chocolate-covered waffles and drink mint tea long into the evening.

"You must always treat yourself after a hard day's work," his mother would say. "There's no such thing as too many waffles if you've worked for each one."

Spurred on by the memory of her words, Theo set to work on the broken typewriters. The sooner he fixed them all, the sooner he could get out of the cellar and tell Bastien what he'd discovered.

Pretending to be asleep was an easy thing to do. Bastien had grown quite skilled in teaching his body to stay still and silent when Monsieur Xavier stalked through the dormitory.

Tonight was no different. Bastien kept one eye scrunched tightly, but slowly opened the other to find Monsieur Xavier lingering in the dormitory, walking back and forth between the rows of beds over and over again. What was he looking for? The director had already destroyed his book and Bastien had kept his notebook well hidden away from the director's prying eyes, hadn't he?

Eventually the director left. When enough time had passed and the dormitory was still, Bastien scrambled out of his bed, taking his long nightshirt off to reveal his normal clothes beneath. After sliding his notebook out from under the floorboard, he crept towards the door. Worry filled Bastien from head to toe; he hadn't seen Theo all day and they were meant to be sneaking out again tonight. Had Monsieur Xavier done something to him? Bastien had to find out.

Surprisingly, the door was unlocked. Monsieur Xavier never left it open under any circumstances. What if it was a trap? Still, Bastien reached for the door handle, unsure of what was on the other side.

Bastien's heart returned to a normal pace when he saw Theo, sitting outside the door with his lockpick in one hand and a tired, concerned look on his grease-smudged face.

"What happened? Are you okay?"

Theo shook his head. "Follow me." He got to his feet and led them down the staircase in silence. Bastien waited until Theo had managed to unlock the main door again, lead them through the courtyard and climb over the gates. Once their feet landed on the pavement, his questions burst from his chest.

"Where have you been all day? What have you been doing? What did Monsieur Xavier say to you?"

Theo grimaced. "I can't tell you yet. Not here."

They ran to the nearest station and snuck past the on-duty ticket inspector while he argued with an old woman. Bastien and Theo jumped on the first Métro and squeezed into a corner. The carriage was tightly packed, full of children up past their bedtime and adults off for evening adventures. It reminded Bastien of trips to the Pathé cinema, when he'd spend the journey with his nose pressed up against the train window.

Just before the carriage doors closed, the old woman squeezed through the gap, pulling a brown satchel behind her. Ageing hadn't been kind to her; it had dragged her through the years and crept into her bones. Her back could no longer stay upright and it curved over, making her unbalanced on her feet.

The carriage jerked forward as it left the platform and the woman's bag fell out of her weak grip, its contents spilling onto the carriage floor.

Bastien rushed forward to help. He scooped up loose pages like a paper bouquet and saw the face of an old man staring back at him. It was a poster, just like the ones he'd seen in Le Chat Curieux, with a photo and information beneath it. Jacques Joli had hair like threaded moonlight and eyebrows that were in a constant state of shock. He'd last been seen writing in a café near the Place de la Concorde a couple of nights ago, wearing a brown suit and a silver wristwatch, but had failed to come home.

A hand slapped down on Bastien's shoulder. It was the old woman.

"Have you seen my husband?" Her voice was frantic.

Bastien shook his head. "*Je suis desolé.*"

She turned on her heels and walked down the carriage, handing out posters.

Bastien pushed back through the crowd. He couldn't hide the look on his face from Theo.

"What's wrong?"

"Another writer is missing."

Theo inhaled sharply and shuffled closer to Bastien as the train veered round a tunnel bend. "Another possible kidnapping? No, this can't be a coincidence."

"What coincidence?" Bastien's curiosity boiled over and he gripped Theo's wrist. "What do you know? What happened to you today?"

"The cellar is full of broken typewriters." Theo wiped the remaining smudge of ink from his cheeks. "Monsieur Xavier wouldn't let me out until I fixed them all. It took me all day! When I asked him where they had come from, he got angry."

Bastien's thoughts ran like a current as Theo spoke.

"But here's the strangest thing. I found a message on one of them." Theo's voice rose an octave. "The words had been scratched into the metal, like with a sharp fingernail. It said *Help us*."

As instant as a strike of lightning, the connection hit Bastien. The missing writers, the late nights and locked doors, the eyes watching his every step at the orphanage. And now this: a pile of broken typewriters with urgent messages of help scratched into them.

"*Bon sang!*" Bastien's stomach sank. "It's him, isn't it? Monsieur Xavier is the kidnapper!"

The carriage lights flickered and for a moment everything went dark. Bastien could no longer see Theo; he only saw shapes and outlines of figures. It reminded him of the Isolation Chamber and fear rang in his ears like a siren.

Then the metal mouth of the Métro roared and the lights re-illuminated the carriage.

"Bastien, are you okay?"

His eyes focused on Theo's face, yet the fear still rang clear. "Not at all. If Monsieur Xavier is the kidnapper, then he might also be the man who was at my parents' hotel. The man the police could never find."

Theo's hands flew to his mouth. "Then that means Monsieur Xavier could be the one who started the fire!"

Bastien nodded. If he was living under the care of the man who had killed his parents, then he could no longer deny the thoughts that had clawed at him for so long. "Maybe he's not really an orphanage director. Have you ever wondered what happened to Monsieur Dupont?"

The train pulled to a sharp stop at the next station platform and Bastien watched Madame Joli vanish through the doors. He imagined her returning to an empty house later. It wasn't fair, how good people could lose so much.

"Sometimes." Theo fiddled with his fingers as though he suddenly didn't know what to do with himself. "I never believed he abandoned us. He was a kind soul."

"What if Monsieur Xavier got rid of him and took his place?"

"He arrived just after you did, and he's watched over you like a hawk ever since." Theo nodded. "We've all noticed it. Haven't you?"

"I thought I was being paranoid, but you're right. What if he followed me?" The train veered round a sharp bend and its wheels screeched, the noise tearing right through Bastien.

"But why?" Theo replied. "If it's true… If he killed your parents, then what else does he want from you?"

"I don't know yet, but it's time to stop being so afraid of him." Bastien said this not just to convince Theo, but himself too. "We're going to find out what he's doing and why, and how to stop him before another writer goes missing. Or worse."

Theo agreed. "We'll need proof."

Bastien thought about the police who had carried out the hotel enquiry. They hadn't dug deep enough into what had happened that night. Well, he and Theo would. "If the typewriters are in the cellar, then maybe the writers are in the orphanage too, right under our noses."

Theo shivered. "Why is he doing this? It doesn't make any sense."

Bastien's voice trembled yet it was strong and full of fight: a musketeer's spirit to hide the worries that knotted his stomach. "I don't know, but we'll get to the bottom of it. For the writers and for my parents. But we must be careful. He can't know we're onto him."

"He won't," Theo said. "Tomorrow, we'll start our investigation. Tonight is reserved for another adventure."

Yet the weight of what Bastien now believed to be

true was heavy on his mind. How could he have a night of fun when he was consumed with terrible, torturous thoughts?

"*Oups!* This is our stop." Before Bastien could protest, Theo pulled on his arm and dragged them through the carriage doors just before they closed.

9

THE WINTER FAIR

Emerging from the Métro, Bastien tried to focus on what he could see in front of him. The Grand Palais rose up to meet him; such a spectacular building demanded to be noticed. It was held up by towering, white stone columns and statues crept out of its stone face, covered in a thin layer of frost. What looked like hundreds, perhaps thousands of people were climbing the stairs to the grand entrance, in a great hurry to escape the cold. But even with such a buzz surrounding him, Bastien's thoughts were stuck on repeat.

The message on the typewriter was undeniable proof of Monsieur Xavier's guilt. It tied him to the missing writers, but Bastien knew he'd need more than that if he was not only going to expose the director, but connect him to the hotel fire and his parents too. If Bastien wanted justice, he needed further answers, and he needed to be smart about getting them.

"Why is the whole of Paris and their great-grandmothers here?" Bastien asked. "What are *we* doing here?"

Theo led the way as they weaved in and out of the large crowds moving in unison towards the gates. People moved like waves, flowing into the street from the overcrowded pavements. Bastien didn't really feel like being in such a large horde. He didn't really feel like an adventure any more.

"It's the Winter Fair!" Theo grinned at Bastien. "This is my surprise! You must've come here before? I visited with my parents every year!"

Happy memories flooded Bastien's mind as it all came back to him: eating silver snowflake biscuits with his mother, riding the Ferris wheel ten times in a row, and sneaking a sip of his father's mulled drink when his back was turned – it had been sharp and sweet and spicy all at the same time. But the things he'd just learned were souring his wonderful memories. He'd never get to visit the fair with his parents again. And if Bastien was right, that was all Monsieur Xavier's fault.

"It's a great idea but I'm not sure I'm feeling up to it," Bastien said. "Not after everything we know now."

"I understand." Theo's face dropped slightly. "I just thought it might do us some good. To remember the fun we used to have and that we can *still* have fun."

As Bastien listened to Theo, something shifted in him. Just like that first magic sip of his father's sweet and spicy drink, Bastien felt the fizz of excitement. Theo was right. Monsieur Xavier had already ruined so much. "But we don't even have tickets?"

"That won't stop us." Theo grabbed Bastien's hand and, together, they ran away from the crowd, not stopping until they were halfway down a side street, partly hidden by the remaining leaves of the honey locust trees. Winter's touch had begun to turn them into skeletons.

"What's your great plan then?" A shiver of cold made Bastien hunch his shoulders up to his ears.

"We climb up onto the ledge and sneak in through there." Theo pointed to a large half-opened window jutting out from the stone wall. It was eight feet up, but wishing for something so badly could stretch limbs and conjure extra height.

"Are you sure you can do that?" Bastien knew how Theo didn't like his feet to leave the ground.

Theo nodded unconvincingly. "It's not that high."

"Come on, then," Bastien said. "I'll go first. I'm taller than you and definitely less scared."

Once a hobbling, elderly couple had vanished around the corner, Theo cupped his hands together like a trapeze net and Bastien lifted himself up carefully, trying to keep his weight even.

"All good?" he asked.

"Fine." Theo swallowed a large gulp of air. "But make it quick."

With the extra height that Theo gave him, Bastien stretched as far as he could and, standing on the tips of his toes, he felt his fingertips brush the window ledge. Fluffy snowflakes fell on his head, disturbed from their resting place.

"Almost…there."

Bastien felt along the ledge for something to grip onto, but his fingers were so numb from the unrelenting cold that he couldn't be sure if his hold was tight enough.

Through the window, delighted shrieks pierced the air like a needle. Bastien thought about how many times he would ride the Ferris wheel and just like that, his imagination began to slowly spin as he pictured his head bumping against the clouds.

"*Vite!*" Theo hissed, his breath short.

Not knowing if his skinny arms would buckle under the weight, Bastien spread his fingers out wide and pushed himself upwards. Adrenaline kicked into gear and, with a shove from Theo below, he pulled himself onto the ledge and through the window, landing with a thud on the floor beyond. He looked around to check it was safe and realized he was in a storage room. It was crammed with boxes of various shapes and sizes; an unremarkable room that no one would notice them sneaking into.

Bastien leaned out of the window. Theo stood at the edge of the pavement, his eyes fixed on the ledge. How was he going to get up here without any help? Suddenly, Theo charged forward, running head first at the wall. The bottom of Bastien's stomach fell away as he watched Theo kick his feet against the wall and spring up into the air. His hands scrambled for purchase but, finding nothing, he fell back down onto the pavement.

"Wait a second!" Bastien rummaged around in the storage room for something, anything that could help. He opened a box which was full of red and white ribbons. This would have to do.

"Grab hold of this." Bastien unravelled the ribbon

and held the end tightly as Theo climbed up it. His friend pulled himself over the window ledge and they fell to the floor in a tangle of flailing limbs.

"I really need to invent shoes with springs." Theo stood and brushed himself down. He stuck out his arm and helped Bastien to his feet. "Come on. I can smell waffles."

Despite the fact he could no longer feel his fingertips, Bastien knew he would have scaled the snowy peaks of Mont Blanc if a spectacle like the Winter Fair awaited him at the end. Inside, the palace's main hall had been completely transformed into a winter wonderland.

Underneath the glass dome, a snow-blue Ferris wheel rotated slowly between great fir trees that looked freshly plucked from the forests of Norway. There was a carousel, a snow-sleigh toboggan ride and, in the middle of all the excitement, a gleaming ice-rink full of people skating hand-in-hand.

"It's magical," Bastien whispered. His eyes marvelled at every detail, taking in the sights and smells. Instinctively, his hand reached for his notebook in his trouser pocket. The leather was turning rough on the outside and the pages were worn, but he scribbled furiously. He had to capture the beauty of this place.

Theo followed his nose and wandered over to the rows of wooden huts selling everything from roasted chestnuts to gingerbread men and glazed brioche buns. Bastien stuffed his notebook away and hurried after Theo. The Winter Fair was buzzing with the noise of a thousand people and he didn't fancy navigating it alone.

A familiar smell stopped him in his tracks.

"Wait a minute," he called over to Theo, whose tongue was already stuck to an ice sculpture. Bastien slipped into a stream of people walking from one hut to the next, and jumped out at a small wooden stall. A young girl with a woolly hat, the colour of silver tinsel, stirred a huge vat, adding handfuls of spices and fruit.

Bastien bent over the vat and inhaled. The spice tickled his nose and he did his best to hold in a sneeze.

"Here," the girl said. Bastien looked up and saw the kind smile on her face before he noticed the mug she held in her hands.

"I'm sorry, I don't have a centime on me."

The girl's laugh was kind. "No money necessary. This one's on the house, just don't tell my father." She winked and pointed behind her to where a man was standing, stirring a metal pot of coconut milk and rice.

Bastien stared down at the mug. "*Merci…*"

"The name's Fatou," the girl grinned.

"*Merci*, Fatou," Bastien smiled. "What luck it was to follow my nose to your stall."

Theo couldn't quite believe their luck either, for his eyes lit up like a Christmas candle when Bastien returned with the steaming mug.

"How did you get that?"

Bastien shrugged. "There are still good people in the world, we just don't come across them often."

"*Santé!*" They took sips in turn, careful not to burn their tongues. It tasted just as Bastien remembered and it warmed every part of his body.

"I could drink this every day."

"Your teeth would rot just like Monsieur Xavier's," Theo teased.

Bastien passed the mug back to Theo. "Let's not talk about him any more tonight."

He didn't want to think bad thoughts any longer. Bastien was at the Winter Fair with his best friend. Tonight they would enjoy themselves, but tomorrow would bring a new type of plan: finding out how to prove the awful director's guilt.

After Theo had inspected the Ferris wheel to ensure it was structurally sound, they snuck onto the wheel as many times as they could get away with until a security guard chased them out of the queue. Luck struck when Bastien found a shiny franc on the floor. They bought enough sweets to fill their pockets before sneaking into an empty wooden hut at the back of the fair. Bastien emptied his haul onto the floor and out flowed a waterfall of sugar: mint bonbons, sugar syrup chestnuts, violet candies, marzipan balls and chocolate truffles.

For a while, the only sound was their lips smacking.

"I wish we could stay like this for ever." Theo collapsed onto his back, clutching his stomach.

"We won't find proof that Monsieur Xavier is a kidnapper if we can barely move," Bastien burped; an overindulgence of sugar fizzed in his stomach too. "From now on, we have to be alert."

"You're right," Theo conceded. Still, he unwrapped another piece of nougat and popped it in his mouth. "What about your story? Have you found enough inspiration to finish it for LeGrand?"

"I don't know." Bastien dropped the empty sweet wrappers and pulled out his notebook. "My mind's been elsewhere ever since that night at the bookshop. I think there's a different story that's waiting to be told, about what's happening to the writers and what that might mean for my parents. That's the story I've started to write. We just need to figure out what's going on."

Bastien flicked through his scribbles until he found an empty page and wrote down everything they'd learned so far.

"Well, I think LeGrand will love any story you write," Theo said.

"I hope so." Bastien smiled at the thought of seeing his name on the front of a book. "If he likes my story, he might buy it and we could have enough money for all of us to buy our own house."

Theo sat upright, grinning madly. "Could we have one with enough room for a workshop?"

"You can have whatever you want," Bastien promised.

Theo got to his feet and helped Bastien up. Time always passed at double-speed outside the orphanage. It was approaching eleven o'clock as the boys weaved their way through the crowds and down the steps of the Grand Palais.

On the train back, Theo slumped against Bastien's shoulder. His sugar rush had worn off and he slept soundly, despite the twists and turns of the carriage descending into the tunnels.

Bastien was more awake than ever, though. He'd written page after page, and his notebook was quickly filling up with the mystery of the missing writers and his parents. He was sure that they were linked, like constellations in the night sky, and Monsieur Xavier was an asteroid, destroying everyone and everything in his path. He thought of Jacques Joli and his poor wife, and Delphine de la Reine. And he thought of his parents – about what had really happened to them that night at the hotel. He put down the pen and stared out through the carriage window into the shadowy depths of the Métro tunnels.

Since the summer, his life had often felt like travelling in the dark with no clear destination. But now he had a purpose: to find the missing writers and uncover the truth about his parents. Had they been Monsieur Xavier's first targets? Why was he kidnapping writers now and what was happening to them? Did the same fate await them too?

Bastien picked his pen back up, ignoring the tingling feeling in his fingers. A little hand ache wasn't about to stop him now. He wouldn't rest until the answers were as clear to him as the flashing neon signs of his city.

10

THE EAST WING

The next day Bastien's need to write plagued him like an itch that couldn't be scratched. His imagination was in overdrive. The story of his parents and the whereabouts of the missing writers had knocked on his brain, demanding to be investigated.

And so Bastien wrote in every snatched moment. No longer did he hide his notebook under the floorboard – it now went everywhere with him. Theo had stitched a secret pocket in the lining of Bastien's trousers with his trusty sewing kit, which he'd found months ago in the darkest depths of Chef's kitchen cupboards. She never bothered to lock them and always looked the other way whenever the boys pilfered the odd biscuit.

"Now you can hide it *on* you," Theo had said, proudly admiring his handiwork.

That evening, Bastien chopped wilting tomatoes in the kitchen. Monsieur Xavier had appointed him as Chef's assistant and so, each night before dinner, Bastien sliced vegetables with a blunt kitchen knife and stirred soups the colour of sewage water. He'd only just wiped juice from his cheeks, the result of an exploding tomato, when a thin, bony hand on his shoulder almost sent his world crashing down around him.

It was Chef. Her arms were laden with saucepans and pots and the look on her face was wild enough to scare even the gargoyles of Notre-Dame. She'd once had a face as fresh as a flower, but working under the new director had doubled her frown lines.

"Monsieur Xavier wants to see you in his office."

"I'll be on my way once I've finished helping you," Bastien replied, trying his best to sound unfazed although his insides had turned to scrambled eggs. He lowered his head and continued to chop the mushy tomatoes into quarters. If dinner wasn't ready on time, Bastien would be in trouble all the same.

Chef prised the kitchen knife from his fingers and gave him a soft look. "He wants to see you immediately. I'll take care of the rest. Go on, go, before he gets even angrier."

Bastien left the kitchen and walked up the stairs. He passed the dormitory, wishing he could hide under his bed, but he steeled himself and walked to the end of the hallway, jumping over bits of broken rock from the second floor's crumbling staircase.

The second floor had long been declared out of bounds. According to Timothée, part of the roof had caved in and almost hit him on the head last summer. Since then, no one had dared to climb the stairs, for fear of being crushed. When Monsieur Xavier arrived, Timothée had made the mistake of asking him if the director might fix it. The director had picked him up by the leg and told him that no boy was to climb that staircase.

Now, standing at the foot of the stairs, Bastien couldn't believe he hadn't thought of it before. The second floor could be hiding any number of Monsieur Xavier's dark secrets. There was enough room up there to hide the kidnapped writers. He fished his notebook from the secret trouser pocket and made a note to find a way to sneak up there soon.

Remembering Monsieur Xavier was waiting for him – and waiting only made the director angrier – Bastien opened the door to the east wing and stepped into what looked like the Hôtel Ritz. All of the government money which should've been spent on winter clothes for the boys, edible ingredients and proper bedding had in fact been used to expand and luxuriously furnish the director's wing.

The cold concrete tiles turned to thick carpet under Bastien's feet, while the usual cracked, grey walls were covered in glossy crimson-red paint and fine pieces of art. Bastien stopped at a painting of rolling lavender fields and pressed his finger against it; a forbidden act which made it all the more exciting. The dried flecks of purple paint felt bumpy under his fingertip and he felt a small thrill to see and feel colour again in a place so grey. Yet the fact that all this existed only for Monsieur Xavier to see reminded Bastien that fairness didn't exist in the director's vocabulary; he mocked the very idea of it.

At the end of the corridor, Bastien stopped outside the office door. Hanging on the left wall was a new portrait of Monsieur Xavier, wearing a crisp white suit and lying on a chaise longue. Red and white roses surrounded his feet and in his lap sat a tiny black kitten.

Monsieur Xavier looked at the kitten with an expression somewhere between adoration and constipation. It was so extraordinarily bizarre, Bastien didn't know whether to be sick or howl with laughter.

"Enter!" a thunderous voice boomed from the other side of the door, reminding Bastien where he was. "I can sense you lingering outside like bad breath."

Bastien steadied his nerves. He'd been inside the office more often than the other boys, each time doing his best to survive the director's interrogations about Bastien's sub-standard sweeping and lack of attention during classes. But this time was different. Now Bastien had his own suspicions. He didn't know what Monsieur Xavier wanted from him, but if the director was hiding any evidence of his guilt – the red-lined cloak Alice had mentioned, or belongings from one of the kidnapped writers – then they'd almost certainly be locked away in his office.

He opened the metal door and found Monsieur Xavier sitting behind his large, marble desk. Everything in the office was black, from the midnight-coloured fur rug and black floor tiles to the shutters, which were closed. Tall, church-style pillar candles lined the room, casting an eerie glow.

Bastien risked a quick glance around the office. It was surprisingly spotless, as though it had been recently cleaned.

"You wanted to see me, Monsieur Xavier?"

"Yes," the director said sharply. "I've heard some concerning rumours about you."

"You have?" Bastien did his best to stay straight-faced. He wanted to confront Monsieur Xavier with everything he believed to be true too, but he told himself to be patient. He would find out the truth in other, less obvious ways.

"I'm sure you know by now that stories are strictly forbidden in the orphanage."

Monsieur Xavier was fishing and, as much as Bastien wanted to bite, he refused to be caught on the director's hook.

"Yes, I'm aware," Bastien replied obediently.

"Then why am I hearing about stories after lights-out?"

Monsieur Xavier rose from his leather chair and Bastien quickly scanned the shelves before the director's body blocked his view. The books were all brand-new, arranged neatly and in alphabetical order. Except for one. *The Secret History of the Catacombs* was upside down and its spine was cracked cleanly in half.

"Bastien!" Monsieur Xavier stood over him, like an eclipse. "What do you have to say for yourself? I know you're telling stories and writing them down in that secret notebook of yours."

"N-no, that's not true." Words bumped into one another on Bastien's tongue. His mouth was clumsy with lies, so he closed his lips and took a deep breath. All the while, his notebook pulsated against his leg. If that's what Monsieur Xavier had been looking for all this time, it didn't make any sense. Why would he be interested in his notebook? "I wouldn't dare to defy your orders. The book, the one you burned, was my only possession."

"You'd do well to bite your tongue before you backchat me, boy!" Monsieur Xavier barked. "Empty your pockets now."

Bastien dug his hands into his trousers and prayed Theo's secret lining would stay put. Thankfully it did. All that fell out of his pockets were a few crumbs.

Monsieur Xavier snarled, the veins in his neck bulging as thick as tree roots.

"You're hiding something. I know you are the precious son of Margot and Hugo Bonlivre. Surely you're desperate to share more stories with the world, *non*?"

Bastien flinched. He didn't like his parents' names in Monsieur Xavier's mouth. The man spat them out carelessly and without meaning, as if they weren't the greatest people to have ever lived. If the director had really had something to do with their deaths, then how dare he speak their names at all!

Bastien rolled his hands into clenched fists. "You knew them, didn't you?" Anger, the blistering, boiling kind, took over. "What do you want with me? Why did you follow me to the orphanage?"

For a brief moment, a crack appeared in Monsieur Xavier's stern expression, but as quickly as it had appeared, it vanished. He walked back to his desk and sat down, kicking his feet onto the desk.

"You'd better think twice before you make such accusations," he replied coolly. "As well as flattering yourself so highly as to think *I* would follow *you* to this place." A croaky chuckle escaped from the director's lips. "You don't want to make an enemy out of me, Bastien."

Weren't they already enemies though? Monsieur Xavier disliked every boy in the orphanage, but there was a special place in his heart, full of contempt, just for Bastien.

"I'm watching you. Very closely." Monsieur Xavier snapped a pencil cleanly in half with one hand and pointed to the door with his other. "Get out."

Although he still hadn't found anything that clearly tied the director to the missing writers, Monsieur Xavier's reaction had been enough to confirm Bastien's suspicion that the director had surely known his parents. As much as Bastien wanted to fire questions at Monsieur Xavier like pellets, fear controlled his limbs and so he ran out of the office, down the staircase and through the corridor, far away from the man who'd ruined his life.

At bedtime, the director's bitter words echoed in Bastien's head. Even an extra slice of baguette at dinner from Fred hadn't cheered his spirits. How did Monsieur Xavier know about his notebook? It was becoming increasingly clear that he knew much more than Bastien had ever realized. Just what was Monsieur Xavier after?

Bastien fidgeted in bed, his mind full of nightmares. He had been happy once and so surely he would be again. It was simple mathematics, wasn't it?

He looked over at Felix, who was sitting at the foot of

his bed with a sullen look on his face. On his second day as director, Monsieur Xavier had confiscated Felix's guitar and whittled it down to a small wooden stick. Now, Felix's hands moved up and down in the air, plucking on imaginary strings that he longed to play again. He needed cheering up as much as Bastien did. Tonight's story would be for him.

"Gather round, *les potes*," Bastien whispered – he had to be more careful now that Monsieur Xavier knew about the bedtime stories. "Tonight is a tale about the power of peace. How enemies can unite through the simplest of things. Like music."

Felix perked up at the mention of music. It had been so long since he'd heard a song, even a single note. He closed his eyes and listened to Bastien.

"Some people are born with talent, a special skill that makes them unique. Most people learn their talents through hard work and dedication that leaves their skin calloused but their heart happy. Felix's talent was, conveniently, a perfect combination of both. For Felix possessed the rare quality of being naturally gifted but as tireless in his dedication to perfecting his craft as an Olympian.

"He'd been born into a family where music was the most important language. He learned to read sheet music before

reading his first book. Felix's choice of musical mastery was the guitar. He plucked the strings with a delicate precision that moved even the most sceptical of audiences. Soon, he was invited to perform every night with the city symphony orchestra, a rare honour to be gifted to a guitarist. Each night ended with a standing ovation and red roses at Felix's feet.

"But when the fighting arrived, it came fast and furious and split the city in two. Felix was separated from his mother and sisters, and he joined his father at the battlefront. Music became a distant memory as the sounds of the city turned violent, but still Felix carried his guitar with him everywhere, strapped to his back. He hadn't yet given up hope. He remembered his grandmother telling him about the power of music to heal and cure all ills.

"The city was sick, and perhaps music was the right antidote.

"One violent afternoon, Felix climbed the barricades. He ignored the pleading shouts of his father and removed the guitar from his back.

"He started to play a song; one so enchanting that the whole city stopped to listen.

"Weapons clattered to the floor, enemy lines blurred and, by the end of that same song, the streets were awash with the waving of white flags.

"Felix could no longer tell who was on which side, for they were all brothers in song, singing along to the melody of peace."

"*Magnifique*," Felix said, his voice full of wonder. Bastien's words had stirred up a storm inside of him; images of him and Fred listening to music with their parents moved through his mind like a symphony. He'd pushed them to the back of his memory, like abandoned cardboard boxes in a dusty attic, not daring to remember. But remembering felt good, and so he made a promise to himself to do it more often.

"Bravo, Bastien," Fred grinned, ruffling Felix's hair. "Only you could make my twin sound so impressive."

The sound of laughter drowned out Sami's weeping, which he was thankful for. He'd been listening to Bastien's story – not that he'd ever admit it. Sami had told himself he would be stoic and strong until he could find a way out of here. What was the point of stories? You couldn't rewrite life. If that was possible, he would've started all over again a long time ago.

Sami turned in his bed silently, and muffled his sobs with the chewed corner of his blanket. He thought of his father and the words he'd comforted Sami with when he was little. *Nothing dries sooner than a tear*. That might once have been true, but Sami's tears weighed on him like all the water in the Mediterranean Sea. He feared they would never dry.

11
EVIL WITH A SIDE OF STEAK FRITES

Olivier Odieux had eaten at Le Malheur every Monday for the past ten years. The restaurant was a stone's throw away from his house in Montmartre and boasted the best steak frites in the city. Much like his writing, Olivier's talent for cooking was non-existent.

Tonight, Olivier wanted to sink his teeth into fatty, raw steaks. The demands from his editors had grown more frequent. They'd called so often in the last week that he'd instructed Louis to disconnect every telephone in the house. But their orders still rang clear. If Olivier didn't have five stories completed in just over three weeks, then he could forget about his money.

But missing a deadline wasn't his biggest worry.

What kept Olivier up at night was the notebook.

It had long been rumoured after the death of Margot and Hugo Bonlivre that they'd left behind a notebook containing an unfinished story. For the last few months, speculation about the location of the notebook had been wild. Some had suggested it was hidden deep in a vault under the Bank of France; others said the pages of the story had been torn apart and spread across every city in the country. Some had even guessed that the Bonlivres had sent it to England on the back of a carrier pigeon.

Olivier couldn't care less about the story, but he knew that the notebook contained something much more important. The notebook also contained a secret, one that the Bonlivres had discovered about his grand plan. It was the type of secret that could ruin him, and his ambitions, for ever.

"Good to see you, Monsieur Odieux," the waiter said, bowing as though the President stood before him. "Your usual table is ready and your brothers have already arrived."

Olivier nodded and dumped his coat on the waiter's head.

Through the thick cigarette smoke that hung in the air like fog, Olivier saw Xavier and Louis sitting opposite each other, their arms folded and faces stern. He chuckled under his breath, amused at how awkward his two brothers were. They acted as though the same blood didn't pump through their veins.

"*Bonsoir.*" Olivier sat down at the head of the table. The waiter scurried over and filled up a large glass from a ruby-red bottle.

"Good evening, Olivier," Louis replied, obedient as a house-trained dog.

Olivier turned to his youngest brother. "So, Xavier, what news of the Bonlivre boy?"

Louis muttered under his breath. He resented how Olivier seemed to have far more respect for Xavier. Louis had always been the one to organize Olivier's life, everything from booking his lavish lunch meetings to his dentist appointments. Xavier had never run through the city in the rain, with a heavy satchel full of freshly-typed stories to deliver to the printers. But Louis had, more times than he could count.

"Bastien is up to something." Xavier picked up his rare steak and took a bite, his lips smacking and blood dribbling down his chin. "Sometimes at night, I can hear him telling the boys stories on the other side of the dormitory door." Xavier slammed his hand down on the table, the fatty juice from his steak spraying across the table. "It's pathetic."

"I don't care about bedtime tales! What about the notebook?" Olivier swilled the wine around his glass impatiently. "You mustn't lose focus. Finding it is our priority. We have searched for months and exhausted all other possibilities. It *must* be with the boy." He took a sip of his drink; it was sharp and stained his teeth red. "That's why you're at the orphanage. To find it and to *destroy* it."

Louis looked down at his plate and nibbled on a few frites. They were crisp and delicious and he wished that he was with better company to enjoy such a meal. He thought of Philippe and the many meals they'd enjoyed together.

"I know," Xavier snapped back. "I've searched high and low, but it's nowhere to be found. Bastien is starting to grow suspicious too. He asked if I knew his parents."

"You must look harder and faster!" Olivier slammed his glass down on the table and the stem broke into pieces in his hand. A waiter hurried over and set a new glass beside his plate.

"I will find it, brother, I swear," Xavier replied. "I admit, I've been distracted with the kidnappings. It's becoming difficult to find writers. They seem to all be writing together now at a bookshop near the river. They don't go anywhere unless they're in a group."

"Must you talk so loudly?" Louis hissed.

"Calm down, Louis," Xavier laughed. "Why are you always so highly strung? Do you really think any honest types come to Le Malheur? Look around! This is where the criminal underworld of Paris comes to dine and talk of dark plans."

Louis stole a quick glance around the room. To his left, a man spoke in hushed tones to a woman with thick, painted eyebrows and a handbag overflowing with different identity cards. A large group of men with oversized trench coats and slicked-back hair were gathered around a table, counting stacks of banknotes – most likely criminal bosses and their associates.

Olivier leaned forward and Louis watched, gleefully, as Xavier squirmed in his seat.

"Listen to me carefully, *petit frère*. You must find the notebook at all costs. I don't care if you never sleep again. Bastien is hiding it and making a fool out of you. Whether he knows it or not, he is holding my reputation, my plan in those pages. You must look harder."

"I won't let you down." Xavier raised his glass and both Olivier and, reluctantly, Louis joined in.

Olivier grinned like a professional psychopath. "All our hard work so far will not be for nothing. The name Olivier Odieux will live on for ever in the pantheon of the world's greatest men. It shall never be tarnished and we shall live the rest of our lives as rich as kings."

Louis placed his glass back on the table and got to his feet. He'd reached the end of his threshold for tolerating evil tonight.

"Going somewhere?" Xavier asked, his face gleaming with triumph.

Louis faked a yawn and did his best to look convincingly tired. "If you'll excuse me, I have an early start tomorrow morning."

Olivier nodded. "*À demain.*"

Louis slipped on his coat and said goodbye, but Olivier and Xavier were already hunched over their wine glasses, whispering about plans that didn't concern him.

As he walked home that evening, along the Saint-Denis canal, Louis felt himself growing increasingly unsure of his place alongside his brothers. Doubt crept over him like a rash. Olivier had to finish his stories; he needed the money. They all did. But kidnapping writers and stealing from children…was this really something Louis wanted to be part of?

He thought of Bastien. How could Olivier steal his notebook after already taking so much away from the poor boy? Margot and Hugo had been good people. Louis didn't know what they'd discovered, but it had been enough for Olivier to consider them a threat. There was still so much that Louis didn't know for sure, but he doubted his brothers would ever admit to the full extent of their secret scheming or tell him the real reason behind their terrible crime.

Olivier's words played on a loop in Louis's mind as he turned away from the canal, slipping down a side street. *Our hard work.* There had been nothing hard about the awful acts they'd committed. Louis willed his mind not to think about it all, but each day the weight of it grew heavier.

He tightened his scarf around his neck and quickened his pace as his apartment door came into view. The biting fury of winter still raged on, but Louis would've swapped the wonder of Paris for a lifetime of living in arctic conditions if it meant he could take back the part he'd played in ruining Bastien's life.

12

SECRETS ON THE SECOND FLOOR

With Monsieur Xavier now watching him closer than ever before, Bastien wished for eyes in the back of his head. He didn't know how the director had found out about the storytelling, for the boys were as loyal as soldiers. None of them would have betrayed him in exchange for a quick reward. Besides, any reward here would be nothing more than another helping of suspicious-smelling chicken broth at dinner or an extra bar of soap to wash with.

Any opportunity for Bastien and Theo to scour the orphanage for further proof of Monsieur Xavier's guilt was near impossible. The director had taken to random inspections while the boys ate, turning their pockets inside out as they tried not to choke on their food. He checked on them throughout the night at random hours and had even taken to sleeping outside the locked dormitory door some nights, slumped in his office chair.

"Do you think he knows we're onto him? About him being the kidnapper?" Theo had whispered to Bastien as they'd climbed the stairs to the dormitory one evening after dinner.

"Maybe." Bastien cast a quick glance over his shoulder. Monsieur Xavier stood at the bottom of the staircase, his cold eyes staring straight back at him. "We'll just have to be even more careful."

And so Bastien no longer dared to write in his notebook. During the day, he kept it tucked away in his secret trouser pocket and when night fell, he buried it deep under the floorboard beneath his bed.

It exhausted him. How was he supposed to spy on Monsieur Xavier and gather information to prove his guilt, when the director was watching his every move even closer than before?

The second week of December brought with it a dreary, grey mood and even drearier chores. Bastien was polishing Monsieur Xavier's portrait in the east wing; he'd been instructed not to stop until the wrinkles on Monsieur Xavier's forehead were wiped clean. Bastien scoffed quietly at the impossible task. He could polish the painting for an entire week but the director's face would look just as hideous.

The day trickled by without Theo as Monsieur Xavier had stolen him away again down to the cellar. Bastien wondered what his friend would find this time; maybe more broken typewriters and secret messages. But today, Bastien was planning an investigation of his own. The abandoned second floor beckoned to him. If Monsieur Xavier was hiding anything up there, he'd find it.

The office door flew open and Bastien dropped the polish bottle in surprise as Monsieur Xavier looked down at him. From this angle, Bastien spotted a large bogey up the director's nose. He thought it best not to tell him.

"I know it's impossible for you not to behave like a circus clown, but I have a very important phone call shortly and I am not to be disturbed." Monsieur Xavier glanced down at the bottle rolling around on the floor. "Do you think you can manage to not make any noise?

133

If I hear so much as a peep, I'll tie your lips together and you'll never tell another story again!"

Bastien nodded meekly, not daring to meet Monsieur Xavier's gaze. To look him in the eye was to encourage his torment.

"By the looks of it, you're nowhere near finished. My face must sparkle like a Cartier diamond."

"*Oui*, Monsieur Xavier."

The director slammed the door shut and Bastien heard the clomping of his leather boots as he walked back to his desk. A minute later, the office telephone shrilled.

As Bastien turned back to the painting, an idea lit up his whole body. If Monsieur Xavier was busy with his terribly important phone call now, he had time to slip away, unnoticed, up to the second floor. Bastien didn't stop to think about it. Every second was precious. He ran the length of the east wing and closed the door quietly. The decaying staircase unravelled in front of him and Bastien climbed carefully, afraid it might give way at any moment.

The second floor was exactly as Timothée had described: a crumbling mess. Half of the ceiling had caved in, and sharp, broken roof tiles lay scattered across the floor. Bastien looked up and spotted a bird's nest, perched between two half-broken beams. It was made from green moss and inside were a pair of swifts.

A stench of mould and stagnant water invaded Bastien's nostrils. It was enough to make him want to turn back, but he couldn't, not when he needed proof of the director's wrong-doings. He walked along the corridor, only stopping to rip up a handful of mushrooms, which were growing from cracks in the wall. He'd give them to Pascal. Perhaps he could make a soup with them if they were the sort you could eat.

There were two doors, one on either side of the corridor, and an archway right at the end. Bastien opened the door on the right and, to his disappointment and frustration, found no missing writers, nor mountains of typewriters or broken pens. The room was empty, the walls cracked and peeling like dry skin.

The room on the left was full of beds, just like the ones in the dormitory. A thick layer of dust covered bed sheets that were brown with grime. His feet squelched and Bastien looked down; a melting slush of snow and leaves covered the floor. It was no wonder the orphanage was so cold; the windowpane was broken and wind whipped through the cracks, bringing the winter inside.

Why hadn't Monsieur Xavier repaired the rooftop already? Bastien knew it was low on his list of priorities; the director only cared for himself.

The chill forced Bastien from the room. As he hurried down the corridor, the smell of decay grew stronger; even the sewer rats of Paris would have run in the opposite direction. He didn't know how long he had before Monsieur Xavier realized he'd abandoned his chores, but he still had nothing – no clue to the missing writers' whereabouts. Thinking of them, Bastien set his jaw, pinched his nose, and walked under the archway.

The room opened up into a bathroom, the once-white walls now covered in brown slime. Smashed sinks spouted out water the colour of orange rust and a layer of mildew covered the floor. The bathroom was disgusting, but the perfect place for hidden secrets. No one would ever come here.

Opposite the sinks were rows of wooden cubicles. Bastien opened the first door and the smell almost knocked him off his feet. It reminded him of blue cheese and Fred's armpits when he refused to wash; a deadly combination. Bastien searched each cubicle, one by one, closing the doors behind him with one hand, the other covering his nose.

Frustration weighed heavy on Bastien's shoulders as he opened the last cubicle door. There was nothing here to help him prove his suspicions. No traces of kidnapped writers meant nothing to tie the director to his parents' fate either.

He sat down on the cracked toilet seat and pulled his knees to his chest. Why couldn't a piece of luck fall right into his lap? He knew that he was right about Monsieur Xavier; he felt it deep in his bones. But what good was a feeling instead of actual proof? Most adults traded in facts and evidence and if Bastien had none, no one would listen to him. Who would believe that Monsieur Xavier was a kidnapper and possibly a killer?

Bastien reached into his secret trouser lining and pulled his notebook out, along with a pen from his sock. He wanted to escape from real life for a moment, away from the never-ending disappointments, and lose himself in words.

He couldn't tell how long he'd been writing when the sound of a door slamming broke his concentration.

Someone had just entered the bathroom.

Bastien froze. If Monsieur Xavier caught him, his notebook would be as good as gone. He listened to the footsteps intently, which sounded lighter than the director's usual clomping stride. If it wasn't him, then who was it?

Then a piercing cry echoed around the bathroom.

It was the sound of someone who had been bottling their sadness for a long time. Another cry followed, this one deeper and longer than before. Carefully, Bastien unravelled his legs and stepped down from the toilet. Through a gap in the wooden cubicle door, he peered out at the figure sitting on the bathroom floor.

Sami sat slumped against the wall, his head in his hands as he gulped large hiccupping sobs. Bastien had never heard such a sound before. Apart from the songs Sami sometimes sung in his sleep, Bastien hadn't heard him say anything else.

Bastien shrank back against the cubicle door, unsure of what to do. A quick thought flitted through his mind. If he left now, quietly, he could avoid being seen, but then again, could he really leave Sami all alone and so upset? He knew in his heart that there was only one thing to do: the right thing.

Bastien swung the cubicle door open and it flew back, hitting the wall.

Sami's head snapped up. The skin around his hazel eyes was puffy and his cheeks were wet. He looked up at Bastien with a mixture of confusion and annoyance.

"I didn't mean to disturb you," Bastien said, wincing at his noisy self. "I was hiding too, I suppose. Are you okay?"

Sami stared at him, his mouth open as though he was about to speak. Bastien's eyes widened in anticipation, but Sami's head simply rolled back down to his chest, shrugging off the question.

Still, Bastien persisted. Maybe here, away from the others, Sami would open up to him. "I know it's hard here, but the orphanage is an easier place with the help of friends. A burden shared is a burden halved, *non*?"

Sami looked at Bastien again, his eyes trailing downwards this time. Bastien followed his gaze and realized that Sami was staring at his notebook. It was poking out the top of his trouser waistband.

"Please," Bastien stuttered, "it's nothing. It's just something that's important to me. *S'il te plaît*. Please, Monsieur Xavier can't find out."

How could he have been so careless? He didn't know if he could trust Sami yet; how could he trust someone he'd never had a single conversation with? For all Bastien knew, it was him who had told Monsieur Xavier about the storytelling. Each evening, Sami would simply roll over in bed, choosing not to take part. Had he hated Bastien's stories that much?

Sami got to his feet and stepped forward. He pointed at Bastien, then back at himself, bringing his index finger to his lips, and in a flash, fled from the bathroom. Bastien turned around, dazed and slightly whiplashed. What had just happened?

Sami was still a stranger, but now Bastien realized they had something in common: they were the keepers of each other's secrets.

At dinner, Chef's food trolley rolled into the table and hit Bastien on the ankle. The sharp pain pulled him from daydreams of his unexpected meeting with Sami. Why hadn't Sami talked to him? Bottling up feelings was dangerous; a delicate alchemy that could explode at any time.

"Eat up," Chef said, placing a bowl of ratatouille down in front of him. "You boys are lucky this evening. I managed to get some fresh vegetables from the market."

"Can't we have some of what he's having?" Felix nodded in Monsieur Xavier's direction, who was dipping forkfuls of salmon into a pot of creamy butter sauce.

"There must be leftovers," Pascal added.

Chef sighed, casting a quick look over her shoulder. "I shouldn't…" She fished a couple of golden-coloured brioche buns from her apron pocket and flung them across the table to Pascal. "Make sure you share," she whispered. "And don't let Monsieur Xavier see. He'll have my head on the chopping block."

The dining hall doors burst open and Theo hurried to his usual seat, black grease staining his hands and an exhausted look on his face. The other boys were too busy trying to steal the buns away from Pascal to notice.

"More typewriters?" Bastien asked, reluctantly eating a mouthful of stewed vegetables.

Theo nodded, wiping the grease down his trouser leg. "Another five to fix, but no markings this time. I don't know whether that's a good or bad sign."

Bastien grimaced as he forced down another spoonful. "I snuck up to the second floor this afternoon, but there was nothing there apart from broken beds and bad smells."

Theo frowned. "How did you manage to get away? Monsieur Xavier has eyes in the back of his head just for you."

"He had an important phone call. He said he wasn't to be disturbed."

"I wonder who he was speaking to. Did you hear anything?"

Bastien shook his head, annoyed at himself for not having thought of eavesdropping. "I ran out of the east wing as fast as I could. I didn't think I'd have long looking around the second floor."

"I can't believe we haven't found any evidence yet." Theo frowned, a wave of doubt rippling across his face. "Are you completely sure Monsieur Xavier is guilty? Not just of the kidnappings but of what happened to your parents too?"

"I feel it," Bastien insisted. "Just like I know when a sentence sounds right, or when you crack an invention. It's in my gut. Everything points to him. I need you on my side."

"Hey, you two!" Pascal interrupted, sliding two squished chunks of brioche down the dining table. "Eat up."

Theo tore into the brioche. "*Desolé*. I don't doubt your feelings. You know I'm with you. I'll do whatever it takes so we can expose him and get out of this place even quicker. Your story might help free us, but proving

Monsieur Xavier's guilt will take away his freedom for good. We just need to up the stakes."

"We will." Bastien forced a smile. As he chewed on the sweet bread, he couldn't find much joy in this rare treat. It tasted as sour as a mouthful of lemons. Other than the typewriters, they'd found nothing else to prove they were right about Monsieur Xavier being the kidnapper. Without proof, Bastien's suspicions would stay just that: nothing more than a feeling, no matter how strong. There'd be no justice for anyone, no justice for his parents.

He couldn't let that happen. He was a part of his parents' story, still alive and determined. Their chapter may have ended too soon, but he would make sure it was told properly. It was, Bastien felt, his duty.

13

AN UNEXPECTED VISIT

I t took Bastien ten minutes to put on his socks the next morning. They'd turned hard with dirt and he winced as his toes crunched and crackled. To cut down on costs, Monsieur Xavier had now instructed Chef to wash the boy's clothes every other month. December was an unwashed month and so their shirts were stained and their trousers smelled of stale sweat.

"Do you want to swap shirts with me?" Clément stood at the end of Bastien's bed. "I'll trade you a jam blob for a coffee stain."

Clément had arrived at the orphanage the night before. He'd been escorted by two policemen with faces like thunder, who'd found him in the most expensive suite in the Hôtel de Vendôme, after a call from a confused receptionist. A quick search of his pockets revealed a wad of banknotes so thick, the first police officer mistook it for a loaf of bread. Clément insisted he'd found the money outside the Moulin Rouge, but he was a street kid, tough as old boots with his set jaw and voice like gravel. The police took one look at his scruffy blond hair and the scar on Clément's collarbone and made up their mind.

"Makes no difference to me." Bastien shrugged. Clément threw on his newly-traded shirt and headed downstairs for his first breakfast in the dining hall.

Bastien looked over at the next bed, where Sami was pulling on his shoes. He looked up and their eyes met for a second. Since the other day, Bastien had hoped a friendship could form between them, yet today Sami still looked back at him with a blank expression and nothing to say. Any recognition of their one-sided conversation in the second-floor bathroom had disappeared. Sami stared at Bastien as though they were strangers.

It was a sight for disbelieving eyes when Bastien saw people walk through the gates that afternoon. He was in the courtyard with Theo, Sami, Felix and Fred; they'd been tasked with cleaning the front-facing windows and had been polishing vigorously. At the sound of footsteps, they turned around, their backs straight and chests puffed out.

When the faces came into view, Bastien recognized them instantly. Alice and Charlotte waved enthusiastically, their golden hair spilling out from underneath their woollen hats.

He should've been excited to see them again, but Bastien's stomach only tightened with fear for what Monsieur Xavier would do if he saw them. Bastien didn't want them to come face to face with the director. Charlotte had lodged a complaint against him after all, and Alice had already been turned away from the orphanage gates several times. What would happen when he realized she'd returned again? Now that Bastien knew what Monsieur Xavier was capable of, he didn't want them to become his next victims.

"*Coucou!*" Charlotte called.

"We wanted to come and see you properly this time." Alice smiled. "Papa is looking after the bookshop – it's been so busy lately with all the writers working together there. He sends his love."

"You shouldn't be here," Bastien whispered. He needed

to protect them from Monsieur Xavier. He'd been planning to tell Alice the truth about the orphanage, about how difficult it had been living here, but now he swallowed down those words. He couldn't lose the only other people he loved like a family. The more Bastien found out about Monsieur Xavier, the more he wanted to keep everyone he cared about far away from him, and far away from this place.

"*Quoi?*" Alice frowned. "What do you mean?"

Before Bastien could reply, he heard the slam of the orphanage door.

"*Bonjour,*" Monsieur Xavier called out in a sickly-sweet voice that sounded as natural as a barge horn, which horrified Bastien and the boys. They'd never heard him sound so pleasant before.

Unsurprisingly, Monsieur Xavier's pleasantries were as short-lived as a sneeze. His face dropped like a rollercoaster as he walked over to Charlotte and Alice.

"I thought I told you that you're not on the visitor list," he snarled at Alice. "How did you even get through the gates? You're trespassing!"

Bastien squeezed the rag cloth in his hands. He didn't want his friends to get in trouble, or worse. Not because of him.

"The gates were already open. We're here to see Bastien." Alice walked straight up to Monsieur Xavier and crossed her arms to match the stern look on her face. "Maman went to the neighbourhood town hall and was reliably informed that there are no visitor lists for city orphanages. We have a right to be here and *I* have a right to see my friend."

They all watched Alice in fearful awe. None of them had ever heard anyone speak to Monsieur Xavier like that before.

The director's face darkened like a storm cloud on a clear day. "Well, *I* am the director of this orphanage and my word is final."

Alice growled like a lion in response and Charlotte tugged her back. "Monsieur, we've brought books for the boys. Last time we saw Bastien, he said you didn't have anything to read here."

Monsieur Xavier's eyebrows knitted together. "And when did you last see him, exactly?"

Bastien glanced at Alice in a panic and thankfully she understood what he couldn't say: that Monsieur Xavier definitely didn't know about their late-night bookshop visit.

"Maman," Alice interrupted. "Why don't you show

148

the director what we have with us?"

Charlotte took a step forward but Monsieur Xavier flicked out his wrist as though she was a flea trying to jump on him.

"Let me stop you right there, Madame. I'm afraid we don't accept donations." He looked at his watch, already bored by their presence. "Now please, I must insist you leave. You are obstructing the smooth running of this facility."

Charlotte glared. "These books are mine and I am free to give them to whoever I want." Her voice was fierce. "Perhaps you should think about treating these poor boys better? I'm sure the officials at the town hall won't be happy about the state of this place."

Bastien watched the battle play out on Monsieur Xavier's face. The director squirmed, then clutched his hands together in a half prayer. "You're absolutely right. Please do forgive me. I'm quite overstretched here and a fair few things are coming apart at the seams. What we lack in riches, we make up for with enthusiasm." Monsieur Xavier pointed to the entrance, as the boys looked on, their jaws wide open. "Do come to my office and I'd be happy to log these books. I think a library room will do the boys good."

Lies spewed out of his mouth like red-hot magma. Bastien suspected that even the pretence of kindness was eating Monsieur Xavier up on the inside.

"Very well," Charlotte said. "Lead the way."

Bastien's chest tightened with concern as he watched Charlotte follow Monsieur Xavier up the steps. Surely he wouldn't do anything to hurt her while Alice was here in the courtyard? Bastien tried to keep his worries at bay, but the dangerous depths of Monsieur Xavier's double life washed over him once again.

The orphanage door closed with a bang. Fred dropped his rag to the floor and suggested a game of rock marbles to Felix and Theo. They ran off towards the gates while Sami sat down by the half-frozen pond.

Alice turned to Bastien with the look of a tired schoolteacher.

"Right, Bastien, what exactly is going on? Don't you dare think about telling me anything but the truth." She crossed her arms. "Everything is not okay here, is it? I bet the catacombs are in a better state than this place!"

Bastien knew he had to tell her the truth. He didn't want to put any of them in danger and he definitely didn't want Alice to lose her parents too. But Alice was one of the smartest people he knew. Maybe she could help him and Theo prove Monsieur Xavier's guilt.

Bastien called Theo over from the gates and the three of them huddled together.

"Firstly," Bastien said, "have you heard any news about Delphine?"

"Nothing yet," Alice said. "A couple of Maman's friends are even sleeping in the bookshop when it gets late. They're simply too frightened to go home."

Bastien shook his head in sorrow. Monsieur Xavier's wickedness had spread far beyond the orphanage, his callous grip reaching into the cobblestone streets of the city. How much longer would this go on if he wasn't stopped?

"Anyway, don't change the subject," Alice huffed. "Tell me what's going on right now."

"We think that Monsieur Xavier is responsible for kidnapping the writers."

Alice said nothing for a moment, only twirling the ends of her hair round her fingers, a nervous habit that Bastien recognized. "What proof do you have?" she asked, finally. "And what would he want with a bunch of writers?"

"I found broken typewriters in the cellar," Theo

explained. "One of them had a message asking for help scratched into the side, so we think the writers must be near the orphanage."

Alice pulled on her hair so sharply that a couple of strands floated to the floor. "Have you seen Delphine?"

Bastien shook his head. "We haven't found them yet, but if the typewriters are in the cellar then they can't be far."

Alice steadied herself. "You could all be in danger!"

"You're right," Theo replied, "but where else can we go?"

"And I can't leave until I find out the truth." As much as Bastien wanted freedom, he couldn't walk away just yet. Not too long ago, the orphanage had been somewhere he'd desperately wanted to escape from, but now Bastien knew its four walls were hiding secrets – secrets he was meant to uncover.

"Remember when you mentioned the suspect in Delphine's disappearance?"

Alice nodded.

"What you said made me think about my parents, and a man at the same hotel as them who the police never managed to question." Bastien paused; he knew what he said next would make Alice's head explode. "I think they're the same man."

Alice ground her jaw, her eyes focused and unblinking. "Then that means…"

Bastien nodded, the truth of everything he'd been through now spilling from his lips. "Monsieur Xavier came to the orphanage just days after I arrived here. Ever since then, he's been obsessed with making my life a misery. He constantly watches over me, more than the others, and he's always sniffing round my possessions. He burned my parents' book and he's trying to get his hands on my notebook, though I don't know why."

"It's true," Theo added quietly.

Alice's mouth fell open. Bastien wasn't sure if she was going to shout at him or cry. Her eyes twitched, blinking back fast-forming tears. "You can't stay here a second longer!"

"I have to." Bastien turned away. "I know it's dangerous, but I need answers. I have to understand. I think if I keep my notebook hidden from him, so I still have something he wants, nothing bad will happen to me. Or any of us."

"Why didn't you tell me all this that night at the bookshop?"

Bastien finally looked up at Alice; the look of hurt on her face sent shocks of guilt through him. "I didn't know what it meant then," he admitted. "I still don't really know now. But the one thing I know for certain is that I don't want to put you or your parents in danger. You're like family to me. I couldn't bear the thought of something happening to you and it being my fault."

Alice sniffed and jabbed her finger into his chest. "We *are* your family. So you better not keep anything from me ever again, Bastien Bonlivre. Promise?"

"Promise."

Alice smiled and wiped her face with her sleeve. "Well, what are we going to do?"

"We have a plan," Bastien said, decidedly. "And we need your help."

"We do?" Theo didn't sound so sure.

"You said so yourself. We need to up the stakes." Bastien looked around the courtyard quickly; Monsieur Xavier hadn't yet reappeared. They were safe. "Alice, can you come back to the orphanage on Saturday morning by eight o'clock? Bring your parents and the police. Even anyone from the town hall who can help get rid of Monsieur Xavier. By then, we'll have the proof we need to lock him up for good."

Alice nodded at Bastien's instructions, but Theo still looked bemused.

"That's only two days away!" Theo scratched his head. "How can you be so sure we'll find proof?"

"I'm surprised you didn't think of it first. We're going to break into Monsieur Xavier's office."

Theo's eyes lit up. They were well experienced in breakouts by now, but this would be their first break-in.

"You're sure about this?" Alice said. "It sounds too dangerous, especially after everything you just told me. What if we tell my parents? Maybe they can help?"

"No!" Bastien lowered his voice. "Promise me you won't. Monsieur Xavier will get spooked. You saw how he acted earlier. I already feel guilty for involving you." He gently squeezed her hand and hoped she'd understand, no matter how irrational he sounded. "This has to stay between us, for now. I can't put your parents at risk. If Monsieur Xavier killed my parents, he needs to be brought to justice so he can't hurt anyone else."

Alice's face softened. "I'll do it." Her round, blue eyes filled with tears. "I'm sorry you've had to live here, Bastien. I wish you could've stayed with us."

"There's nothing you could've done before, but now you can help us to make things right. For the writers

155

and for all of us in here. And for my parents." Bastien put his arm around her.

"I won't let you down."

The bang of the orphanage door reverberated behind them and the boys hurried back to their window-cleaning just before Charlotte emerged, scurrying down the steps with Monsieur Xavier following closely behind.

"It's time for us to go, Alice," Charlotte called. She hurried over to Bastien and hugged him tight. "We'll see you soon." Then her voice dropped to a whisper. "I shall go back to the town hall tomorrow and lodge another official complaint. I won't leave until I speak with the head *préfet*."

Charlotte kissed Bastien on the cheek and led Alice towards the gates.

Bastien waved goodbye to Alice. He knew she didn't want to leave him here, but she had a part to play in their plan and he was sure that she'd scale the July Column one-handed if it meant helping him. He was luckier than he realized to have friends as fierce as Alice.

Monsieur Xavier locked the gates and let out a lethal burst of laughter.

"Did you really think you'd jump into their loving arms and they'd sweep you off to a new life?" He leaned forward, his stale coffee-breath tickling Bastien's face. "Remember that the only people who cared about you are long gone." Monsieur Xavier clicked his fingers and the boys filed back through the orphanage door and into the dining hall.

"Was that your friend who visited?" Fred whispered to Bastien, as they sat on the end of the bench.

"*Oui*, Alice is my oldest friend."

"She's the bravest person I've ever seen," Fred said. "Standing up to Monsieur Xavier like that takes courage. I wish I could be like her."

Bastien looked up and down the dining table, watching the others talk among themselves. Theo was discussing the mechanics of building a secret stove behind Pascal's bed, and Robin and Felix were arm-wrestling Clément and Timothée for the extra pastry crust that Chef had given them. Despite the daily difficulties that came their way, they still found a way to survive.

"Alice is brave, but so are you," Bastien replied. "We're all braver than we know."

14

A THIEF IN THE NIGHT

"**T**ell us another story!"

"One about me, pretty please, with a *cerise* on top."

The boys had taken to bribery to be the next star of Bastien's story. Clément had offered a handful of boiled potatoes at dinner, and Pascal promised him a bowl of home-made mushroom soup. But Bastien refused them both.

Since Alice's visit yesterday, he and Theo had kicked into planning mode. Bastien had stolen an extra box of matches from the kitchen for his reading light, as they'd need a strong light to help illuminate the path to Monsieur Xavier's office after midnight.

Theo was tasked with collecting a handful of small metal typewriter parts from the cellar. He'd need a much longer lockpick if he was going to break into Monsieur Xavier's fortress of an office, but when he snuck down between chores the cellar door was closed and the lock too high for him to reach. He would have to wait until tomorrow when Monsieur Xavier gave him more typewriters to fix.

Waiting one more night to break into Monsieur Xavier's office felt impossibly long, but Bastien knew they had no choice.

"I'll get what we need by tomorrow night," Theo had reassured Bastien. "Don't worry."

Bastien was thankful for his best friend and so tonight's story would be dedicated to Theo.

"*Écoutez!*" Bastien whispered and the boys came rushing like a pack of hyenas. Pascal leapfrogged over Timothée's back and landed with a soft thud at the foot of Bastien's bed.

"Watch where you're going!" Timothée clutched his arm. "My bones are fragile."

Pascal rolled his eyes. "You're not street-performing any more, Timmy."

"Will both of you shut up?" Felix moaned.

Silence fell and expectant, excited eyes stared up at Bastien. He cleared his throat.

"Tonight is a story about inventing your own happiness."

"On a balmy summer's evening, Giles Larouche arrived at the Paris Exposition Universelle with ambition so bright, a lighthouse keeper on the white cliffs of Dover reported a sighting of a silver light stretching over the water.

"The cleverest minds from all over the world had gathered to share their cutting-edge inventions, and at twenty years of age Giles had created something greying inventors could only dream of. He'd worked on the mechanical wings for a year, holed away in his small apartment in Lille. Now he had made the trip to the capital and he was finally prepared to share them with the world. What he definitely hadn't prepared for was to fall in love.

"Baya Kateb had worked long days ever since she'd been a small girl. Even after her parents passed away, she spent every day in their workshop, carrying the family business by herself. Baya was the finest jewellery maker in the whole of Algeria's Kabylia region and people flocked, from home and abroad, to buy a brooch, a pendant or a beautiful pair of earrings made of silver and coral. It was said that each creation was magic in its own way.

"One day, an elderly French woman appeared outside the workshop. She'd travelled far to purchase one of Baya's pieces for herself, and was so impressed that she offered to pay for Baya's passage to Paris, where she would display her work at a grand exhibition.

"Baya didn't want to leave her country behind. When she packed her suitcase that night, she did so with a determined scowl on her face. She would go to Paris and make as much money as she could. Then she would return to Ath Yenni and her little workshop on the highest hill.

"Or so she thought.

"The journey brought Baya to the white-stone pavilion at the Paris exhibition, where she showcased the beautiful jewellery she'd made: earrings that changed colour according to the temperature and waterproof coral necklaces that would keep the wearer bone-dry.

"As she sold her jewellery to crowds of delighted customers, and ignored those who gave her strange looks, Baya noticed a particular face pass by her stall every hour. Finally, when she had sold her last silver brooch, Giles summoned his courage. He walked right up to her and held out his hand. To her surprise and his delight, Baya took it.

"Under the night illuminations, the pair danced in each other's arms and promised they'd never be parted.

"Their love story was one of great joy and the day that their son Theo came kicking into the world was the best day of their lives. Theo was their best invention and their family life was full of the type of laughter that made breathing impossible.

"Later, when his parents were gone, it was their laughs that Theo missed the most. He clung onto the last time he'd seen their faces; waving goodbye to them when they'd set off to test his father's new aircraft. But that memory wasn't enough to last him a lifetime. He wanted more.

"Theo drew a picture of his parents, of their bright, inquisitive faces. He shaded in his father's constantly arched left eyebrow and delicately drew the laughter lines that rippled across his mother's face when his father told terrible jokes.

"He worked day and night in their old workshop, only stopping when fatigue forced his eyes shut.

"On the fourteenth day, it was complete.

"Theo placed the automaton on the kitchen table. The wooden figures of his parents were slightly crooked, but the resemblance was uncanny. He turned the key with a soft click and the figures turned slowly. His parents danced around in a circle, their eyes fixed on each other, and the sheer happiness Theo felt pulled him to his feet.

"He danced around the automaton, in sync with his parents' movements, and didn't stop dancing until the *moon surfaced in the sky.*

"Even though hard times were ahead, Theo knew he would never really be alone. Not while his parents still danced by his side."

The dormitory was silent long after the story's end, until Theo jumped to his feet. There were bubbles of tears in his eyes, but even through his blurred vision he saw Bastien smiling right back at him. The other boys applauded too, careful to not make too much noise. Monsieur Xavier couldn't ruin such a story: for tonight, they'd all lose themselves in dreams where they danced with their parents.

"Bravo, Bastien the Brilliant," Theo said in a choked voice.

Theo didn't scare easily, but investigating the rattling, shaking sound that stirred him required more courage than he currently possessed. The sound had pulled him from his best dream in a long time: he'd been dancing with his parents onstage at the Palais Garnier in front of a sold-out audience.

There it was again, the same rattling sound, followed by a groan. He couldn't ignore it now. Someone was here, sneaking about in the dormitory.

Theo crawled to the end of his bed and dared to look. In the dark, he could just about make out a pair of familiar battered leather boots sticking out from underneath Bastien's bed. What was Monsieur Xavier doing?

Theo tried to shout but his throat had closed up like a flower bud. He tried to move but fear had turned his body to stone.

The triumphant yelp that Theo heard next only confirmed that Monsieur Xavier had struck gold. Theo strained his neck, under the security of his blanket, but darkness was on the director's side, camouflaging his movements.

The dormitory door slammed shut, but it was only when he heard the sharp click of a key in a lock that Theo found he could move again. He shrugged off his blanket and ran over to Bastien's bed.

"Wake up!" He shook Bastien, who was asleep face-down on the mattress. "It's Monsieur Xavier."

Bastien groaned and opened his eyes a fraction. "What is it? What about him?"

"He's stolen your notebook!"

Waiting outside Monsieur Xavier's office the next morning, the hope Bastien had felt yesterday now drained from his body like cold, dirty bathwater. With the morning light on his side, he'd checked underneath the floorboard and tipped up his bed and turned the sheets inside out, hoping to find his notebook caught in a tangle of blanket. But Theo was right.

It was gone; the last gift from his parents, his story about the missing writers and his chance to earn a better life. And now that Monsieur Xavier had his notebook, what would become of Bastien?

Bastien tried to take note of the various locks on the door, to tell Theo later, but his mind flitted like fireflies, unable to land on anything for long. He imagined storming into Monsieur Xavier's office and demanding his notebook back with all the authority of the President. Instead, he settled for a timid knock, and the door opened inwardly as Bastien stepped into the lion's den.

"Who dares interrupt my morning routine?"

Monsieur Xavier sat gleefully at his desk with his feet resting on top. He held a pair of nail clippers, and bits of nails littered the floor. Bastien suppressed a grimace. He went to sit down, but Monsieur Xavier raised his hand like a stop sign.

"What are you doing here?"

Bastien glanced at the director's desk. It was empty apart from some pharmacy bottles and an ashtray overflowing with cigarette ends.

"Something has gone missing in the dormitory." Bastien was careful with his words; Monsieur Xavier surely knew what he was after. "It was one of my personal belongings," he admitted. "A notebook."

Monsieur Xavier's left eyebrow shot up to his hairline. "All of your personal belongings were confiscated under my management. If your notebook has been taken, then you shouldn't have had it in the first place, should you?

Think of it as a natural rebalancing."

"I know I shouldn't have kept it, but it's more important to me than you can imagine," Bastien begged. "Do you know where it is?"

"All of this for a notebook?" Monsieur Xavier snarled. "I should send you to the Isolation Chamber for a month for such dishonesty!" His face was as straight as an iron rod; the director wasn't going to give anything away.

"I know it's been stolen," Bastien dared, his pulse quickening.

"How my heart bleeds for you!" Monsieur Xavier rubbed imaginary tears from his cheeks. Bastien suspected that his heart was, in fact, not bleeding, for it was as hard as stone.

"You are sharing a room with the most verminous children in the city," the director continued. "Of course it's more than likely that it's been stolen."

Bastien bit his tongue. Monsieur Xavier had no right to talk badly about any of the boys. Why should they be automatically considered dishonest thieves? None of them had asked for a rough start to life, yet they all had more honesty in their little fingers than Monsieur Xavier possessed in his whole body.

Bastien shifted back and forth, uneasy about how this conversation was spiralling.

Monsieur Xavier dropped his feet to the floor and leaned forward, his face a picture of wicked delight. "Whatever you're so desperately looking for, rest assured it is long gone."

Bastien knew this was a battle he was destined to lose, but desperation clung onto his every word. "Please. I *need* it." In that very moment, he thought of the last conversation he'd had with his father, about how he'd keep the notebook safe. But he'd failed.

"Silence! Get out of my sight and get back to your chores, otherwise it's a month in the Isolation Chamber." Monsieur Xavier's lips curled at their edges in a menacing clown-like smile. "I have work to do."

Monsieur Xavier waited until he no longer heard Bastien's footsteps. When the boy's pitiful pitter-patter had disappeared, he reached for the phone. Finally, he had in his possession the very thing that had sent him to the orphanage in the first place: the notebook containing the truth that threatened Olivier's plans. What Margot and Hugo had found out, they'd entrusted to Bastien. And their foolish son had been none the wiser.

Now the truth would stay hidden, as buried as the hundred-year-old skeletons in Père Lachaise cemetery. Olivier's grand plan would continue unhindered all thanks to him. Perhaps now, he'd even be given a starring role in the plan.

Monsieur Xavier's spider-leg fingers tapped against his desk as the phone dial tone hummed. As he waited for Louis to answer, the same smug thought repeated through his mind. Louis was scared of the dark, which was unfortunate, because Monsieur Xavier was about to send his oldest brother, and the notebook, underneath the city.

Louis felt a wave of desperation so strong he wished for a lifeboat. As soon as he'd received the call from Xavier, he knew that the dirty work of delivering and disposing of the notebook would fall to him. After running around the city on Olivier's behalf, Louis had finally arrived at the orphanage to be frog-marched through the hallway by Xavier, into his office, and down the ladder that led into the catacombs.

The darkness in these tunnels drowned Louis. He'd always hated them, but Xavier and Olivier were creatures of the night. As boys, they'd run around the city looking for one of the many secret entrances into the network of maze-like tunnels. Xavier, in particular, had been obsessed with tracing where the paths of the old limestone mines and the skull-lined tombs of their royal ancestors met.

But, for Louis, each step was like walking blindly towards a cliff edge.

He walked through the dense tunnel until he came to a small cave opening, feeling as if the skulls in the walls were watching his every step.

Something rough scraped against his cheek and Louis flinched.

A laugh and a flicker of light appeared right next to him. "You still scare so easily, brother."

"Why did we have to come down here?" Louis stepped into the light of Xavier's flaming torch. He could almost remember the time when he and Xavier had felt like friends, but the memory was just out of reach. Now all they shared was a strong dislike for each other.

Xavier noticed the quiver in Louis's voice and a smirk flashed across his lips. "The tunnels are all part of the plan. You have a job to do."

Dread rose in Louis like a tsunami wave. "Which is?" His brothers always expected him to clean up their messes, but he was the last to know about them. The authority that big brothers usually possessed had skipped Louis.

"You must take the notebook to Olivier in Montmartre," Xavier instructed.

"Surely we can just destroy it now?" Louis asked. "Have you looked inside?"

"No!" Xavier's command cut like a sweep of the guillotine. "Olivier's instructions were clear. He wants the notebook untouched until he's read it. He needs to understand just how much Hugo and Margot knew before he continues with his grand plan."

"And what exactly is this grand plan?" Louis chanced.

Xavier simply stared at his brother like his ears were sprouting cauliflowers.

"That is on a need-to-know basis," he replied eventually. "And you certainly don't need to know anything."

Anger stirred in Louis like a pot of hot fondue. Why did his brothers expect him to do everything when they wouldn't tell him the truth?

"If you're not going to tell me, why don't you deliver the notebook instead?"

In a sudden swooping motion, Xavier grabbed Louis by the collar of his shirt, lifting him high into the air.

Louis's legs dangled helplessly above the ground; a marionette controlled by his master.

"You will do as I say, brother. Olivier has trusted me to instruct you and you mustn't forget that, if you fail, I will leave your body for the rats to feast upon."

Louis's shoulders sagged. He would do what his brothers had instructed, as always – what choice did he have?

Xavier dropped him to the ground like an empty sack of coal, picked up the torch and removed the notebook from his pocket.

"Time is of the essence, Louis. Follow the tunnel on the left. It will take you past the writing cavern. From there is a shortcut to Montmartre. Olivier expects you by nightfall."

Louis shone the light over his wrist. His watch read a little after four o'clock in the afternoon. The thought of journeying through these dark, damp tunnels for hours was uninviting.

"And you're certain it's quicker this way?" he asked. "Can't I just take the Métro?"

"Don't question me, Louis. I know these tunnels better than you do. They are a faster and safer way to travel. Now, off you go." Xavier pressed the notebook into his free hand and pushed Louis into the left tunnel mouth. "Safe travels, *grand frère*."

Fuming quietly, Louis started down the tunnel. He didn't want to be here, but Olivier and Xavier didn't care about his feelings. They didn't care about anyone but themselves.

He held the torch aloft and quickened his pace, repelled by the thought of Xavier's smirking face.

As soon as he got to Montmartre, Louis was finished with them both. This was the last time he'd ever do the dirty work for his bad brothers.

Above ground, Bastien and Theo discussed their plan for the twentieth time over Friday's dinner of greying mince and uncooked carrots. Bastien's anger was still raw, but he needed a clear head if he was going to get his notebook back. He chewed on the tough meat, his mind simmering with anticipation.

"Tonight is the night," Bastien said, shuffling closer to Theo so the other boys wouldn't hear. They all had bigger noses than a group of gossip-loving grandmothers, and if they smelled even the faintest waft of a plan brewing, it would spiral out of control. Bastien and Theo were doing this for all of them, to get out for good. Nothing could go wrong.

"Go over the plan one last time, will you?" Theo asked. "I want to make sure it's seared into my brain!"

"The red-lined cloak will tie Monsieur Xavier to the missing writers. You look for that and anything else that could belong to Delphine or one of the other writers. Hopefully, something will lead us to where he's keeping them. I'll search for my notebook and anything else that might be related to my parents."

The thought of finding the truth about his parents and getting justice for them fuelled Bastien. He imagined Monsieur Xavier being led away in handcuffs. Suddenly his dinner didn't taste as disgusting as it usually did.

"We move after midnight?" Theo crunched a carrot in his mouth.

Bastien nodded. "We wait until after Monsieur Xavier's final inspection. When he's gone, we'll make our way to his office."

"And there are six locks on his door?" Theo's brow furrowed, lines of concentration stretching across his forehead.

"At least six." Bastien stole a glance over his shoulder at Monsieur Xavier. The director was slumped forward in his chair, plates of untouched food on his table that Chef would collect and throw away.

"My new and improved lockpick will be up to the task," Theo said, assuredly. "I managed to pocket some metal parts down in the cellar earlier. Monsieur Xavier didn't notice a thing! We're going to get him."

Bastien nodded. He felt Monsieur Xavier's guilt as clearly as his own heartbeat. Everything was connected, but the why and what of it still escaped him. Why had the director been at the same hotel as his parents? What had he wanted from them that night? Bastien hoped the answers were somewhere in the office.

Theo raised his chipped mug in the air, and Bastien smiled, raising his own.

"Here's to finding the truth," Theo declared.

"And to freedom, for all of us." Bastien clunked his mug against Theo's and they drank the sour curds as though it was the finest cow's milk in France.

Sami wasn't an eavesdropper. He was an honest person, and had spent each of his sixteen years treating others with the same kindness that his parents had taught him. But when he heard whispers during dinnertime, his ears pricked up and the muscles in his arms tightened.

Sami had lost something too, something precious that he'd dreamed of every single night since Monsieur Xavier had stolen his belongings when he'd arrived. Sami needed it back; it was the only reminder he had of his father, and he was sure that it was in Monsieur Xavier's office.

He knew every boy in the orphanage had their own desires and secrets, but Sami could no longer live like this. His mother and sister were still at home in Morocco, and each day was time he would never get back with them. A rare smile flashed across his face as he thought of home, the warm sand between his toes and the waves of the Atlantic Ocean. It was as quick as a blink, then he turned back to his dinner, forcing the last spoonful of mince down.

Bastien and Theo were going to help him escape, whether they liked it or not. Tonight, Sami was taking back what was his and escaping the orphanage for good.

18

THREE'S A CROWD

Time dragged its heels. The hours after dinner passed so slowly, Bastien felt like each minute moved backwards. All he could do was toss and turn in bed. He was impatient at the best of times, but waiting to go and get his notebook back and find the proof they needed was like being locked in a room with a pile of chocolate éclairs labelled *Do not eat*; the nearness of it was almost impossible to ignore.

The four hours between lights-out and Monsieur Xavier's final midnight inspection were torture. Excitement and nerves pumped through Bastien's body in equal measures. Still, he waited until he could be sure the director was no longer lingering outside the door.

He counted the minutes until it was twenty past midnight and finally kicked off his blanket. With his reading light in hand, Bastien crept over to his friend's bed. Unsurprisingly, Theo was already sitting up, waiting for him.

"Ready?" Theo asked.

"Definitely."

They'd snuck out before, as stealthy as spies, but now, when it mattered most, Bastien stumbled into a bed frame. He heard Robin stir and placed a finger over his own lips.

"*Chut*, little one," Bastien whispered.

Robin's eyes flickered with drowsiness and he turned on his side.

Bastien felt a pang of guilt for keeping the rest of the boys in the dark, but the proof of Monsieur Xavier's guilt as the kidnapper, and killer, would set them all free. Surely they'd forgive him and Theo for sneaking around when they no longer had to live under the director's reign of terror.

A figure loomed large at the door, stopping Bastien in his tracks. Had they already been caught? He stepped forward and his reading light illuminated the figure.

Sami stood with his arms folded across his chest.

"I'm coming with you." The boy's voice was a firm and confident whisper.

Bastien almost forgot how to speak; he was so shocked at hearing Sami talk. "Where do you think we're going?" Bastien had to play this carefully. What if Sami took their lockpick and made off into the city? Their plan would be over before it had started.

"To Monsieur Xavier's office," Sami replied calmly. "I overheard your conversation at dinner."

Keeping his face a blank slate was a difficult task but Bastien willed his eyebrows to remain unraised and unsuspicious. "You were eavesdropping?"

"It's hard not to when his mouth is so big." Sami pointed at Theo, who instinctively covered his open mouth.

Bastien stifled a laugh. "How do we know we can trust you?"

"Monsieur Xavier took something that belonged to me too." There was fire in Sami's voice and each one of his words burned. "Once I get it back, I'm going home."

"Is this a good idea?" Theo looked at Bastien.

Sami rolled his eyes. "Your mouth hasn't got any smaller."

Sami hadn't said much but the words he spoke carried such authority, like an army corporal, that Bastien knew he had no choice. Saying no to him would be an impossible task…and besides, it wouldn't hurt to have the oldest and strongest boy in the orphanage on their side if they crossed paths with Monsieur Xavier.

"Fine," Bastien agreed. "But follow our lead." He dropped to his knees, peering through the crack underneath the door. "Clear."

Theo picked the dormitory lock in seconds; having an audience always made him keen to impress. Together, they crept across the landing and down the corridor, heading towards the east wing. It was deadly silent in the orphanage and even the rats were absent, as if they knew better than to be out after hours.

"What are you two planning to do exactly?" Sami whispered.

Before Bastien could answer, a door slammed shut downstairs and the sound of moaning floated up from the bottom of the stairs.

"*Vite*, in here!" Bastien pulled open the nearest door. Unfortunately, it was the Isolation Chamber. The door barely shut and the boys wriggled in the darkness, their limbs vying for space.

"I think I just stepped on a rat's tail," Theo hissed in alarm. His arm flew up and poked Sami in the face.

"Be quiet!" Sami hissed, retaliating with an elbow of his own. "He's coming."

Bastien blew out the candle of his reading light and peered through the crack in the door just as Monsieur Xavier appeared at the top of the stairs. He leaned against the bannister to catch his breath, his face glistening with sweat.

The director sighed and pulled something behind him. Bastien squinted to see Monsieur Xavier dragging a large black sack in the direction of the east wing, grunting and groaning as he went.

"Bastien," Theo whispered over his shoulder. "What do you think is in there?"

Then a noise came from the sack.

A human-sounding noise.

As quick as it had sounded, the noise fell quiet. Monsieur Xavier huffed and dragged the sack over the threshold to the east wing and slammed the door shut with his right boot.

Bastien counted to ten and stepped out of the cupboard. Theo and Sami spilled out after him in a ball of limbs and insults.

"How can someone so small take up so much room?" Sami huffed, pushing Theo off him.

"You're joking," Theo replied. "I'm not much bigger than the brooms!"

"Stop it, you two," Bastien interrupted. "We've finally caught Monsieur Xavier in the act!"

"What are you talking about?" Sami stared at him blankly.

"Writers are going missing in the city and Monsieur Xavier is carrying a sack that made a human sound. That is *not* a coincidence."

Sami looked at Bastien as though a broom had hit him on the head.

"Bastien's right," Theo said. "I heard it too!"

"We'll explain everything later." Bastien sighed. "Right now, we need to follow him. We need to help whoever's in that sack!"

Bastien relit his reading lamp, the light guiding them towards the door and down the east-wing corridor. He was afraid of what lay ahead, but he couldn't turn back. Not now.

They came to a stop outside the office door and heard a cacophony of commotion inside; bangs and thumps and muffled shrieks pierced the air. Bastien moved closer but Sami pulled him back under the safety of his shadow.

"Wait a moment," he mouthed.

And so they waited.

When the strange sounds stopped, as suddenly as a snapped violin string, Bastien took a cautious step forward. What had just happened inside Monsieur Xavier's office? He stared at the door, the various metal locks glistening in the glow of his reading lamp.

"How can we break into his office when he's inside?" Sami looked at them both in disbelief.

"We didn't think he'd be here," Theo said. "We thought he'd be out in the city."

It was an unexpected problem; how could they search the office? But Bastien wasn't thinking about that right now. All he could think about was the cry of the person in the sack.

"We need to get inside now and help that person, whatever the consequences." Bastien turned to Theo. "Can you open the door?"

Theo reached out and quietly tried to twist the handle, but it didn't move. He tried again, his grip tighter, but it was solid in its refusal.

"He's locked it from inside." Theo drew his new and improved lockpick from his pocket. It had six different heads, the metals all different shapes and sizes. "Good thing I like a challenge. It's good for the brain, trying to achieve the impossible."

Sami rolled his eyes. "This was your plan? You two are completely reckless."

"We're not reckless," Theo retorted.

"We have to help the person in the sack!" Bastien dared Sami to disagree with him. He simply shrugged, a defeat of sorts. Theo turned his back and set to work on the locks that snaked up the door like a train track. This was sophisticated security and he needed to concentrate.

Bastien stepped away and stood next to Sami, who was glaring up at Monsieur Xavier's portrait.

"Why have you never said anything until now?" Bastien asked. "Why didn't you talk to me the other day?"

Sami shook his head, as though the reason was entirely obvious. "Speaking in this place just makes it real. Silence was my way of surviving Monsieur Xavier. But when I heard your plan, I felt hopeful again."

Bastien understood perfectly. Lack of hope could wire a jaw tight shut. But there was still something he didn't understand.

"Why were you so upset that day in the bathroom? Was it about what Monsieur Xavier took from you?"

Sami looked away and shook his head. Bastien knew that some people kept all their secrets locked away in the treasure chest of their heart. Sami wouldn't tell yet, but maybe he would one day. In his own time.

The first lock gave a satisfying click and the other locks followed closely behind, like a snake uncoiling.

"It's worked!" Theo stepped back, his face radiating pride.

Bastien pushed the door open, uncertain of what waited for them inside.

What he didn't expect, however, was nothing.

The office was completely empty.

19
THE VANISHING OF MONSIEUR XAVIER

Mixed feelings of relief and confusion pulled Bastien's thoughts in different directions. He was pleased not to find Monsieur Xavier's soulless gaze staring him down, but the bizarreness of it only confused him further.

How had Monsieur Xavier disappeared from a locked office? And what had he done with the sack and the person inside it?

Bastien rushed over to the window. It seemed the only possible escape route, but it looked out onto the courtyard below from a considerable height. Unless Monsieur Xavier had the aerial skills of a high-wire performer, he hadn't left through the window.

"Where did he go?"

"Impossible," Sami muttered.

"Just like Houdini," Theo added.

It was mind-bending and almost completely distracted Bastien. He didn't know where Monsieur Xavier had taken the person in the sack, or what awful thing might happen to them.

"Let's not forget why we're here." He turned away from the window. "Theo, you search all the cabinets for evidence. I'll take the bookshelves and the desk and look for another way out of here too. He has to have gone somewhere. We can't stand by and do nothing about another kidnapping!"

Sami dropped to his knees in front of a large wooden trunk and wrenched it open. "I'll help you look for another way out of here once I've found what's mine."

Bastien nodded; whatever Sami was looking for obviously meant just as much as the notebook did to him.

Theo hurried over to the steel cabinets in the corner and Bastien walked behind Monsieur Xavier's grand desk. Placing down his light, he opened the top drawer and found a pile of letters tied with red string. The sender's address was one that he recognized instantly.

Le Chat Curieux.

There were at least ten letters here from Alice. What if there were letters here for the other boys too? What else had Monsieur Xavier been keeping from all of them?

Underneath the pile were more envelopes, all addressed from a street in Montmartre. *13, Rue de la Bonne* was written in scrawled handwriting and a red wax seal, of a pen dipped in an inkpot, was on the back of each envelope.

Bastien put down Alice's letters and picked an envelope up from the pile, dated from that summer. He slipped his finger underneath the seal and pulled out a piece of parchment paper. Written in the same scrawled hand, was a single line:

X, finish the Bonlivre job.

Bastien had been searching for proof and now it seemed like he'd found it – but there was no feeling of triumph. Only horror filled him from head to toe as he read the sentence over and over again. *The Bonlivre job* – did that mean his parents? Had someone told Monsieur Xavier to "finish" them? To *kill* them? The anger he felt almost split him open. Someone had casually ordered his parents' death and he needed to know who it was. Who was Monsieur Xavier working for?

"Look!" Theo's shout knocked Bastien from his rage. He turned to find Theo clutching a spotty scarf. "This was in the end cabinet. Isn't this the same scarf Delphine de la Reine was wearing in the missing poster? She was wearing it the night she disappeared!"

"You're right!" Bastien gasped. This was proof, the kind that you could hold in your very hands, that would expose Monsieur Xavier as the kidnapper. And with the note about "the Bonlivre job", they could tie him to Bastien's parents' deaths too.

"Wait..." Theo's voice faltered. "There's more in here."

"What is it?" Bastien closed the desk drawer and slipped the parchment note into his trouser pocket. Hope rose in his throat. "What else have you found?"

In Theo's palm were two silver objects. One was a wristwatch, its hands ticking quietly, and the other was a silver and coral brooch.

"It's Yemma's brooch," Theo said, dumbstruck.

Bastien's heart lit up for Theo. He knew how much his mother's brooch meant to him, but he felt a mix of sadness and guilt too that his own notebook was still nowhere to be found.

"I'll keep them both safe." Theo tied the scarf around his neck and pinned his mother's brooch onto his shirt collar. "Here." He passed the wristwatch to Bastien. "We need to keep an eye on the time."

The watch shook in Bastien's trembling hands. The words on the note kept flashing through his mind. "I found something," he said, his voice no louder than a croak. "There was a note in the desk drawer. Someone ordered Monsieur Xavier to kill my parents."

Bastien fiddled with the strap longer than necessary, hoping the tears pooling in his eyes would disappear. His hands weren't steady enough to fasten the watch and it slipped through his fingers, clattering to the floor.

Sami looked up from the trunk in alarm.

"Everything okay?" So consumed in his own search, Sami hadn't been paying much attention to the conversation around him.

Theo shook his head and squeezed Bastien's hand. "I'm so sorry. But now we are certain, we will make him pay. We have everything we need to send him to prison."

Bastien took deep breaths until he felt his pulse slowing. "You're right," he said, finally, "but I can't leave yet. Not without my notebook and not without finding out where he took the person in the sack." Bastien walked over to the bookshelves, where there were books in pristine condition on all sorts of things: fencing and money-making, politics and, surprisingly, lots of stories written by Olivier Odieux, the same books that Bastien had seen stacked at Le Chat Curieux. He pulled each book out, flicking them open and then running his hand across the shelf behind. Maybe his notebook was here somewhere, hidden in a hollowed-out book. He'd read about such secret inventions before.

On the top shelf, his fingers landed on an old book. The last time he'd been in the office, *The Secret History of the Catacombs* had sat upside down on the shelf. It was in the same position now, a strange eyesore on such a neatly organized bookshelf. Bastien pulled the book towards him and placed it back the right way up.

A tremor rippled under Bastien's feet, and part of the floor sprang up, as though it had grown legs, the force knocking him over. The black floor-tile, which he'd believed to be solid, was now standing up on its edge, revealing a gaping hole beneath.

It was a trapdoor. A secret entrance.

Bastien scrambled to his feet and peered into the hole. All he could see was a wooden ladder, inviting him to climb into the darkness below.

Theo whistled and stepped forward for a closer look. "Now that's impressive." He wasn't scared, but amazed. That was the instinct of an inventor; the owner of a curious brain who preferred to step towards, not away, from unknown danger.

Bastien lowered himself onto the creaking ladder and prayed it would hold. "This has to be where Monsieur Xavier went. The ladder must lead back down to the ground floor and beyond." Another horrid thought crawled under his skin. "What if he's keeping the writers underneath the orphanage?"

Theo met Bastien's horrified gaze. They had to move quickly. Lives depended on it.

Bastien looked over at Sami, who was sitting against the trunk, the contents spilled across the floor. He had a vacant look on his face.

"Are you coming with us or not?" Bastien asked.

What Sami had been looking for was still nowhere to be seen. He suspected that it was elsewhere. After all, Monsieur Xavier was a magpie who stole precious items and kept them close. But Sami wasn't leaving without it, not now. He'd chase the director to the edge of the earth for it.

"I'm coming on one condition," Sami replied. He got

to his feet and kicked the side of the trunk. "That we make Monsieur Xavier pay for everything he's done."

Bastien and Theo nodded in agreement. Sami was still a mystery, but the three of them were now bound together by their need to hold the director to account for every calculated, cruel move he had made.

"Let's go." Bastien grabbed the light off the desk and lifted himself down. He wrapped the string around his wrist and hoped the flame from the reading light would last the descent. The ladder was rough against his hands and the small space was dank and dusty.

"A hidden passage must've been built on every level of the orphanage," Theo called from above.

"There's too many secrets in this place!" Bastien shivered. He was frightened, but spurred on by the thought of the missing writers. What if they were all tied up in sacks down here, left alone in the dark? What about his notebook too? It hadn't been in the office. The longer Bastien went without it, the more desolate his mind became. He glanced down at the watch. The time was approaching one in the morning.

With a final look around the office, Sami walked over to the trapdoor and squeezed himself down the hole. With an almighty creak, he pulled the trapdoor shut and the tile covered the floor again, as though this was just another boring office, full of dusty books, paperwork and pens, and wasn't hiding a secret entrance to the underworld of Paris.

CAVERN IN THE CATACOMBS

Bastien had never felt more grateful to be in the company of others. Without his parents, he'd often felt loneliness creep over him like a second skin, but with Theo and Sami close behind, he felt somewhere close to safe. As safe as he could descending into the darkness, chasing after an evil man.

Like mice scurrying behind walls, they hurried down the ladder, through the brick and wooden foundations of the building until the ladder ended abruptly at the throat of a narrow limestone passage. A chill swept through the passage, snuffing out the reading light. It took Bastien's eyes a few moments to adjust to the new type of darkness. It was unlike any he had experienced before and thicker than a midnight sky. Down here, the darkness enrobed them all like a cloak.

Theo handed Bastien a match from his trouser pocket and with a hiss, the light returned. The flame was strong enough to illuminate a fragment of the tunnel path ahead. Bastien hoped the candle stump would last; without it they would be lost.

"I knew that would be useful for more than just reading." Theo smiled.

Sami stepped in front of them. "Come on, you two. There's no time to waste." He walked into the tunnel and they followed, the ground crunching under their feet. Bastien tried to make sense of where they were. The rock walls were rough and lumpy, as though figures were trying to force themselves out. There was no doubt that they'd climbed down through the orphanage and were now underground. A small shiver, like a spider crawling up his back, passed through his body and Bastien spun the reading light back onto the path ahead.

After a few minutes, the tunnel opened up into a large cave. More tunnels twisted off from the cave like tentacles and in the middle was a pile of bones. The walls were lined with melted candles, some with a tiny flicker of a flame still burning. Bastien was amazed and terrified at the same time. Where were they?

Sami sighed.

"What's wrong?" Theo asked.

Sami didn't reply. Instead, he kicked the ground and a cloud of dust filled the air.

"If you're coming with us, you have to talk." Bastien's voice rose an octave. "We're not in the orphanage any more. We have to work together."

"We're in the catacombs," Sami said, his voice no more than a whisper. "The way through will be complicated."

Bastien had read books about the catacombs, so he knew that underneath the cobbled city streets was death bathed in darkness. His father had told him stories about how nearly 150 years ago, the cemeteries of Paris had overflowed and a foul stench had lingered in people's homes, until they could take no more. Under the cover of darkness, on wooden carts, the dead had been transported to the tunnels to be buried even further underground.

"How do you know?" Bastien asked.

"I used to live here." Sami's eyes dropped to the floor. He didn't want to see the looks of pity or horror on their faces.

"What? In the tunnels?" Bastien had never imagined a fate worse than the orphanage, but sleeping next to the bones of a thousand bodies was unthinkable. How had Sami ended up down here?

"How long were you down here for?" Theo asked.

"The tunnels are a labyrinth." Sami ignored both questions. "There are different layers and levels. You might not always be going where you think you're going."

Bastien shuddered. The thought of getting lost was enough to turn the most seasoned adventurer to a lifetime of sensible decisions.

"How do we know which tunnel to take?" he asked. "Monsieur Xavier could've gone down any of them." Bastien looked at the tunnels, all leading in opposite directions, and realized how clueless and underprepared he was. Suddenly, his confidence felt paper-thin.

Sami grabbed the reading light from Bastien's hand and dropped to his knees in the middle of the cave.

"The ground is unsettled here." Sami traced his finger in a circular motion over faint footprints. "It looks like something was dragged in this direction." He pointed to the far-right tunnel. Its entrance was narrow and carved into the low arch were the words: *C'est ici l'empire de la Mort.*

"Here is the Empire of Death," Theo muttered. "Doesn't sound too appealing, I'll be honest. You're sure Monsieur Xavier didn't go down another tunnel?"

Bastien was full of dread. He heard the scratching of something sharp from the same tunnel, like long nails on skin, and a high-pitched whistle. It sounded like a scream trapped in the air and the noise filled his ears with fear.

"This is the only way." Sami had already headed into the tunnel, his voice growing fainter with each step. "I'm going with or without you."

Theo pulled on Bastien's arm. "Come on. Sami knows the tunnels better than us. I don't want to get lost down here."

Bastien knew Theo was right. He walked quickly behind his friend, as though he was being chased.

The tunnel was shaped like an hourglass, constricting unexpectedly in the middle as though pinched, only to widen again. Scratches covered Bastien's arms from contorting his body through sharp angles and brushing against the jagged tunnel walls.

"I wonder who all of these bones belonged to," Bastien said. "Maybe they're the bones of royalty, kings and queens long gone."

"Or revolutionaries sent to the guillotines," Theo added.

The catacombs mixed the rich with the poor, the good with the bad. Down here, there was no hierarchy to death: bones were just bones.

Then the tunnel narrowed even more, and Bastien's heart sank. There was nowhere to go.

"It's a dead end." He groaned and kicked his heels into the ground.

"Not quite. You're quick to accept only what your eyes want you to see," Sami called. "Come closer."

As Bastien moved forward, the frame of a door embedded at the end of the tunnel came into view. He rushed towards it, dropping the reading light in his keenness to escape. But a strange clacking sound from beyond the door stopped him in his tracks.

"Can you hear that?" Bastien turned around, the hairs on his arms rising. "It sounds like—"

"A hundred fingers hitting typewriter keys," Theo replied, picking up the reading light. He had a good ear for the sounds of machines.

"If he's keeping people down here against their will, then Monsieur Xavier is even worse than I imagined." Sami clenched his jaw.

Bastien took a deep breath and pulled the door open. It groaned, flecks of rust falling to the floor. The clacking sound roared in his ears as he stepped through onto a limestone balcony.

The cavern before him was enormous. Shelves of stone and bone jutted out from the walls, holding piles of books and flickering candles trapped in skulls. The candlelight gave the cavern a dim glow, like a poorly-lit theatre show.

Bastien looked down.

Two rows of desks ran down the middle of the cavern, uniform and exact. On top of the desks were typewriters, surrounded by towering stacks of paper. And behind each desk sat a person, their heads hung low like deflated balloons, as they all typed in perfect unison.

"It's the writers!" Theo exclaimed. "It's really them!"

From up here, Bastien couldn't make out their faces, but he knew that Delphine de la Reine and Jacques Joli had to be somewhere on the cavern floor. He'd followed his instinct and found them.

"What is this place?"

Bastien didn't have an answer to Sami's question. The cavern was unlike anything he'd ever seen before. A large, bronze clock hung on the back wall, the bottom of it swallowed by the creeping rock as though it was trying to eat time. Two stone gargoyles perched either side of the clock, keeping watch on the writers below. A shiver ran up Bastien's spine.

"This is how we beat Monsieur Xavier." Bastien's legs buckled under him. He couldn't quite believe it. "Finally. This is how we get free of him for ever."

Bastien reached out to steady himself against the stone balustrade, his head light with everything he'd discovered in the past hour or so. His suspicions had been right. Monsieur Xavier had killed his parents and gone on to kidnap writers in the city. The man who had vanished from the burning hotel and the man in the red-lined cloak was the same person.

But why had he done this? If Monsieur Xavier had been ordered to kill Bastien's parents, then was the director kidnapping writers for someone else too? Bastien's mind grew heavy and it turned the cavern floor blurry before his eyes. His sweaty palms slipped, unable to find a solid grip.

He grasped at thin air, trying to find anything he could hold onto to stay upright, but it was too late. He slipped right over the balcony edge.

In a moment of fight or flight, Bastien's fingers found

one of the balcony railings. The sea of typewriters roared below as he clung on desperately.

"Bastien!" Theo's voice above him sounded distant and distorted.

His arms ached; he couldn't hold on for much longer. Bastien knew he only had seconds before he fell.

And then he did.

21
THE MISSING WRITERS

Bastien closed his eyes and prayed for wings to suddenly sprout from his back. He steeled himself for an inevitable crash, but instead landed with a bump. A jolt shot up his back, but he was still in one piece. How was that possible when he'd just fallen through the air?

He pushed himself up, but his hand caught on something and a thin line across his finger drew a drop of blood. It was a paper cut, an injury Bastien was quite familiar with. He looked down properly and found himself sitting atop a pile of crumpled papers. Other piles surrounded him, some stretching high up to the cavern ceiling, rising like the Alps. The one he'd landed on was about halfway between the ground and the balcony.

Bastien looked down at the writers, who were still frozen in place, their heads hanging over their desks as they typed. How could they not have heard his scream as he fell? What was wrong with them?

He unfolded a piece of paper next to him. A page from a story with bright red lines slashed through most of the words. Bastien cringed at the rejected tale; whoever had scored through it clearly did not understand the delicate shades of storytelling.

Theo and Sami burst into view, their arms stretched out in equal concern and relief.

"*Ça va?*" Theo asked. "Are you hurt?"

"I'm still in one piece, I think." Bastien moved slowly, worried that a sudden move might cause a paper avalanche.

"Here, take it easy." Sami lifted Theo onto his shoulders and Theo reached forward to grip Bastien's hand. Carefully, they pulled him down onto the cavern floor.

There were thousands of story pages, all crumpled into a mountain of rejection. It saddened Bastien to see the writers' work so easily discarded. Every story was precious, and deserved to be treated as such, not thrown into a dumping ground of unfinished endings.

"How did you both get down here?" Bastien asked.

"There was a ladder next to the balcony," Theo said shyly. "I did mention it when you were dangling up there, but I don't think you heard."

Bastien pulled a face and brushed fragments of rock off himself. "It's hard to pay attention when you're falling through the air."

"Like Alice falling down the rabbit hole," Sami teased.

"So you do like stories!" Bastien said triumphantly.

"Just because I didn't sit at the foot of your bed, it doesn't mean I didn't listen to your tales." Sami shrugged and walked towards the desks. "Come on, there's no time to waste."

The clacking of the typewriters unnerved Bastien, as he worried it could be masking other noises – they'd never hear other people approaching this cavern. Hurriedly, he counted ten writers, typing like machines, robots programmed to tell nothing but stories. Or were they just too afraid to move?

"Hello?" Bastien's voice echoed around the cavern. Only silence met him.

"We have to get everyone out," Theo hissed.

"How can we?" Sami looked around. "There's only three of us and it doesn't seem like they can move. They must be so exhausted." He headed towards the clock wall. "I'm going to look for other exits in case there's a quicker way out of here."

Bastien and Theo split up, walking between the desks, searching for familiar faces. He stopped in front of a table. An old man sat as still as a statue, except for his withered fingers hitting the keys.

It was Jacques Joli. It was unmistakably the same face from the poster on the Métro. But he had changed. His face was drained of life and his silver hair was now the colour of darkened ash.

"Monsieur Joli," Bastien whispered.

Jacques's head rolled forward, as though the weight of his own body was too much for him to take.

"Bastien!" Theo called. "I've found Delphine."

Bastien looked up and saw Theo rushing towards a woman with her long hair tied back.

"Help me. Please." Jacques's croaky voice startled Bastien. The man could barely speak. He and every other writer in the cavern were no longer people, but shells of themselves.

"What is it?" Bastien said. "What happened to you?"

"Stories…thief," was all Jacques could manage.

Disgust grew in Bastien's stomach as he made sense of Jacques's words.

"Monsieur Xavier is stealing your stories?"

Jacques's head rolled forward, a sort of slow nod.

It didn't make any sense. Monsieur Xavier had no use for stories. Bastien knew how much the director hated them and how he'd taken every opportunity to stop Bastien from telling his own. "Who is he stealing the stories for?"

Before Jacques could open his mouth, Bastien felt a hand on his shoulder pulling him back.

"Footsteps! Someone's coming! We need to hide." Sami led Bastien into a fissure in the cavern wall and Theo squashed in beside them just in time.

"Writers of the dark!" Monsieur Xavier's voice filled every corner of the cavern. "It's time for your break. Be back at your desks in thirty minutes sharp. Our leader expects me in Montmartre before sunrise with freshly-typed stories."

The writers slowly stood up from their desks, wobbling on their feet. The ground vibrated and at the side of the cavern a large metal box rose out of the floor into a kind of cage Bastien hadn't noticed before. The writers came to a stop and then the box screeched open, as slow as a stretch.

"It's an elevator shaft," Theo whispered, full of fear and wonder.

Bastien could only watch as Jacques and Delphine stepped into the lift with the other writers. Where were they being taken? And who was the leader Monsieur Xavier had mentioned? Was that who the director had been working for all along?

When the writers were all packed in like sardines, the doors clasped together and a loud sputtering noise sent the elevator lurching into life. It descended into the rocks, disappearing from view.

"Look." Sami nudged Bastien in the ribs.

Monsieur Xavier dragged the mysterious sack into the middle of the cavern before emptying it onto the floor. A red-headed man spilled out of the bag like fish guts, his hands and feet bound by ropes.

"You have been selected to write for Olivier Odieux." Monsieur Xavier stared down at the trembling man. "There is no greater honour."

The surname rang loud in Bastien's brain, as clear as the bells of Notre-Dame. "Odieux," he whispered. "I know that name. He must be their leader!"

Before Theo or Sami could reply, Monsieur Xavier's screeching voice cut through the cavern again.

"Well, are you just going to roll around on the floor or are you going to say thank you? You should be grateful."

The man on the floor rocked himself back and forth. "*Merci.*"

Bastien pressed his nails into his palms. Monsieur Xavier had kidnapped the poor man and now expected him to say thank you? The director was truly delusional.

"You must write one thousand words an hour, no less. If you fail to meet this target, it'll be *your* bones lining the walls." Monsieur Xavier's arm wrenched forward and pulled the man up from the floor. "Remember, there is *nowhere* to hide down here. If you run, you'll lose yourself in the tunnels." He produced a pair of scissors from his cloak and cut the new writer's ropes.

The man swayed as he regained control over his limbs, unsteady on his feet.

"Put these on and follow me." Monsieur Xavier threw a pair of overalls at the man. He unzipped them with shaking hands and pulled them over his clothes, but his foot caught in one of the legs and he fell to the ground.

"Hurry up," Monsieur Xavier hissed.

The man jumped back to his feet as the elevator rose up into the cavern to meet them.

The last thing Bastien saw before the doors shut again was the sneering grin on Monsieur Xavier's face.

Hiccupped breaths, salty tears and bitter anger came spilling out of Bastien as he emerged from the crack in the cavern wall.

"Bastien, what is it?" Theo asked. "What do you know?"

"I recognize the name Monsieur Xavier mentioned."

"Who? Olivier Odieux?"

Bastien nodded as his shoulders shook. "He's a writer. I've seen his books at Le Chat Curieux. There were some in Monsieur Xavier's office too."

"So…" Sami pieced the parts together. "Monsieur Xavier must be working for Olivier. Kidnapping writers to create stories for him?"

"But if these writers are working for him, then why has Monsieur Xavier stolen your notebook too?" Theo asked.

The same question had been whirring around Bastien's brain. "The last time Monsieur Xavier called me to his office, he mentioned my parents. He asked if I was going to carry on telling stories like them, and he thought I was hiding something in my notebook…"

"When I was listening to you two at dinner—"

"Eavesdropping," Theo interrupted Sami, quickly regretting it from the look Sami shot him in return.

"Anyway," Sami continued, "you said you needed to find the connection between Monsieur Xavier and your parents, didn't you?"

Bastien nodded. "He's responsible for what happened to them. The note in his office proves it – someone ordered him to kill them."

"Well, if it was Olivier who got Xavier to kidnap those writers, surely it was also Olivier who ordered your parents' deaths. They must have known Olivier. They must've known he was evil."

Bastien looked at Sami, then back at the rows of desks. Everything washed over him so suddenly that he slid down to the floor, propping himself against the nearest desk leg.

"You're right." Another thought clogged up Bastien's insides like the mushy courgettes they ate at dinner. "They must've left something for me in the notebook about what they knew! The night before my parents left for Cannes, my father acted so seriously. He told me to always keep the notebook safe. Maybe it wasn't just a gift. Maybe I was supposed to be protecting something else?" Bastien half cried, half hiccupped. "But I've failed them."

Theo kneeled down next to him.

"I don't know what your parents knew, but it wasn't this, about the kidnapped writers and their stolen stories. Remember what Alice told us at the bookshop? Writers didn't start going missing until September."

"Then they must've known something even worse," Bastien said, a sob at the back of his throat.

"Whatever they knew, we're going to find out, because we're going to get your notebook back. I promise." Theo hugged him. "You haven't failed your parents, so don't you dare think that for a second longer. We're going to get justice for them and justice for these writers."

"Yes." Sami stood awkwardly, his hands twisted behind his back. "And we'll take back what is ours."

Bastien smiled at Theo and Sami. He was grateful not to be in the catacombs alone. With the help of his best friend, and a new friend, they'd face whatever would come next together.

"Monsieur Xavier said he was going to Montmartre," Sami said. "That's where we should go. He must be delivering the notebook to Olivier along with the stories."

Bastien nodded in agreement, but he couldn't shake his guilt at the thought of leaving the writers behind; it was trapped under his skin like a bee sting. "We can't leave these people here, can we? They're still in danger!"

"I'll remember the way back to this cavern," Sami promised. "I can lead the police here once we're out."

"I promise you that we'll come back for them." Bastien knew Theo meant what he said; a promise between friends was written in stone. Theo stretched out his hand and helped Bastien to his feet. "Now come on, we've got some wrongs to right and a notebook to steal back."

"Let's go and stop Monsieur Xavier once and for all." Bastien gritted his teeth and glanced down at the watch. It was approaching three in the morning but he strangely wasn't tired. He was running on adrenaline. Hopefully it would last.

Sami paced up and down the rows of desks like a tiger locked in a cage.

"What are you doing?" Bastien asked.

"Thinking." Sami looked at him with sparkling eyes,

which told Bastien all he needed to know. He'd never seen Sami glow so bright with determination, but he knew that the best plans shimmered in the dark.

Sami stopped in his tracks and turned to face them. "I know a shortcut to Montmartre."

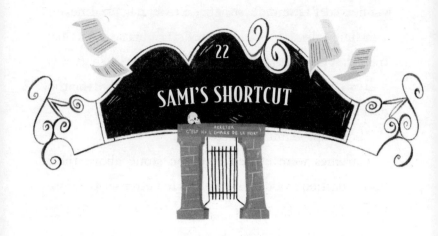

Bastien's heart lurched upwards. Even in the grimness of the cavern, Sami's words struck a match of hope.

"Really? You can get us there quickly?" If Sami knew the way, then they would be able to get back to the orphanage by eight o'clock. Alice was trusting Bastien to turn up with proof of Monsieur Xavier's guilt, otherwise the police would think she was nothing more than a time-waster, a foolish girl playing a prank. He wouldn't let her down. This was his plan and he wasn't going to let it fail. He *couldn't* let it fail.

"Right now we're underneath the Panthéon," Sami replied confidently. "Montmartre is another five kilometres north. If we stick to the north-easterly tunnels that I know, we should save time. Follow me."

Sami walked to the back of the cavern and they trailed behind. Hidden behind the elevator shaft was a small opening. Stone stairs disappeared into the darkness beyond.

"Look up," Sami instructed.

Carvings were etched into the stone above their heads. Bastien stood on his tiptoes to better see the sign. It read *Place du Panthéon*.

"During the construction of the tunnels, they added the names of every street that ran overhead," Theo said. "I remember my father studying the catacomb plans but they always just looked like squiggles to me."

Sami nodded. "I don't know much about maps, but I know the way. If we head in this direction, it will take us to Gare du Nord. The old rail tracks there will lead us straight to Montmartre."

"That's great." Theo's voice wasn't as optimistic. "But Montmartre is a big neighbourhood. How can we expect to find Monsieur Xavier? We have to think logically."

A flicker of a memory, of a crumpled envelope with a red seal, lit up Bastien's brain.

"There was a letter in his office from an address in

Montmartre. Right near the Sacré-Cœur. 13 Rue de la Bonne. Maybe that's where Olivier lives? That's got to be where he's going." Bastien bounded forward, this knowledge fuelling his feet, but Sami pulled him back.

"Wait!" His voice carried a warning. "I will lead the way. I know these tunnels better than you do. I understand your anger – Monsieur Xavier has made us all suffer – but we have to be careful."

Bastien's eyes widened with excitement, or nerves, or perhaps a belly-fizzing combination of both. He repeated his father's mantra, a saying to help him through life, especially the difficult bits: "It's not as if you have to drink the ocean." Whatever Bastien faced, he could overcome it, drop by drop. The path to Montmartre wouldn't be difficult if they stuck together and took one step at a time.

They followed Sami into the tunnel. It smelled of the grime of thousands of long-forgotten bones and Bastien wished that this journey had taken him on a more pleasant-smelling path. But he knew that you couldn't choose an adventure, especially one so unexpected; you could only answer its call.

23

FOOTSTEPS IN THE SHADOWS

Louis hated being alone. He especially hated being alone and desperately lost. He'd survived a war and illness, but he didn't think he could survive another day of loneliness. It gnawed away at him like a flesh-eating bug and walking through the catacombs, completely disorientated and off-track, made him feel more alone than he'd ever felt. He'd given up so much for his brothers: his life, his relationship with Philippe and his entire career. It dawned on him that he'd sacrificed everything for not much in return.

From the time ticking away on his watch, he saw the hours had passed from afternoon to evening, and into the early hours of the following morning. Louis felt as though he was destined to walk these tunnels for the rest of his days. Each dark, damp passage looked the same, and even the red chalk he'd used to mark the path had failed to help him. Louis was lost.

He cursed his brothers. Olivier's pursuit of this notebook was obsessive. What had Margot and Hugo Bonlivre written in those pages that they'd been killed for? And what was worth him losing his mind in the catacombs?

Louis held the flaming torch to the tunnel wall and one of his red markings glared back at him. He was walking in circles. The marks had been meant to guarantee his way out of here, but they increasingly felt like a call for help, proof he'd been here if a search party ever came looking.

Xavier had made the directions sound so simple, but the tunnels were anything but straightforward.

Louis moved the torch and it illuminated a small gap in the wall to his left, barely big enough for him to squeeze through. He hadn't noticed it before. He sighed and stuffed his body through the gap. Hopefully, this was the right direction. He just wanted to give the notebook to Olivier and be done with this all.

The gap opened up into a small cave, and as Louis

pulled himself from the crevice, a sharp, shooting pain took hold of his back. He tried to ignore it but it crept higher and higher until his shoulder blades locked together in protest. Stalagmites rose from the ground, as sharp as skewers, and Louis stumbled in his attempt to avoid them. The last thing he needed were holes in his feet as well as a bad back.

He wanted to hurry, but his body needed rest. The most important thing now was for Louis to make it out of the tunnels alive. Olivier could wait for the notebook a little while longer.

Louis found a smooth-surfaced rock and sat down with his back resting against the cave wall. He propped the torch against the rock and stuffed his thin stick of red chalk back into his coat pocket. Over the years, he'd learned to always carry something that could be used to quickly write down Olivier's great ideas. Louis had experienced enough of them in the most difficult of places: the zoo, the dentist while he was getting a filling removed, even during an audition. Louis had had to cut his song short and follow Olivier out of the opera house.

The city above felt so far away. When this was all over, he would leave Paris and start a new life somewhere. A life without his brothers, where he only answered to himself. He'd lost count of the times he'd told himself this, but this time was different. He truly meant it.

That thought pulled him back onto his feet quicker than expected. Louis could start a new life, on one condition.

That he could get out of the tunnels and survive what came next.

Breaktime was over for the catacomb writers. They walked wearily back to their desks, their hands aching and heads throbbing. Their next break was at sunrise, around five hours away.

Monsieur Xavier watched them, pride pumping through his veins. In just a couple of months, he'd created this army of storytellers. Now Olivier had enough writers to finish the five stories in time and it was all thanks to him. He'd saved Olivier from losing his fortune and protected his grand plan by stealing the notebook. There was no way his big brother wouldn't reward him justly.

He sniffed. A strange smell permeated the air, one he only came across above ground, floating through the dormitory and dining hall.

Monsieur Xavier walked behind the elevator shaft, where the smell was strongest, and ran his finger against the wall. Dust and dried bone covered his fingertips, but an unbalanced smile still rippled across his face.

"I smell children."

Minutes in the catacombs felt like hours. The further they walked into the maze of passages, the further Bastien felt from real life. With every new corner they turned, Bastien saw movement; a flicker of light, a sharp angle or moving shadow that would turn out to be nothing more than a dark figment of his imagination.

Fear had no face but its home was the catacombs, Bastien was sure of that.

The mind games didn't stop there. There were steps that led to nowhere, ascending into walls, and passageways with stone doors that wouldn't open. Bastien tried to make sense of the scrawled writing that plastered some of the walls.

"People leave messages down here to help them find their way back through," Sami explained. It was easy to see why. Everywhere Bastien looked, false promises of escape presented themselves. The tunnels were teasing them.

And then came the cruellest trick of all.

The light went out and the darkness came crashing down.

Bastien carefully retrieved the candle stump from the jar. Its wick was black and smoking.

"It's okay, I've got a spare wick, remember?" Theo mumbled. "That is, if I can find it in my pocket."

"Be quick," Sami said. "The darkness is swallowing us. I don't want to lose my sense of direction."

A high-pitched cry flew down the tunnel. Bastien couldn't tell which direction it had come from.

"Be patient, Sami," Theo said. "This should burn for the rest of the way."

"What do you mean?" Sami's voice curved like a question mark. "That wasn't me."

It took a moment for Sami's words to sink in. They weren't alone in the tunnel. Suddenly, the stuffy air turned ice-cold and Bastien's breaths became short and sharp like a dagger.

There was a hiss and the reading light lit up the tunnel again. Like a camera flash, it illuminated the crooked shadow of a person with a perfectly crooked smile who had crept up behind them under the cover of darkness.

"I'm sure you three realize it's strictly forbidden to be out of bed at this time."

The shadow stepped forward and Monsieur Xavier's face grinned down at them. His lank hair clung to his face like grease on a kitchen pan and his rows of rotting teeth glowed in the dark.

Bastien stumbled back.

"You boys shouldn't be down here," Monsieur Xavier said casually, like he wasn't planning to grind their bones together.

Sami pushed Bastien and Theo behind him and stood firm. "Give back what belongs to us."

Monsieur Xavier took a step closer, his eyes bulging and bloodshot as though he hadn't slept for weeks.

"I must say, I preferred it when you kept your mouth shut, Sami."

Courage found Bastien and he stepped forward, his body now between the director and the boys. "You'll pay for everything you've done. For every life you've ruined with your horrific crimes."

Monsieur Xavier laughed, the echo in the tunnel transforming it into a screech. "Now that's where you're wrong. I'll be just fine. But you three have broken my rules." Monsieur Xavier shuffled closer, parted his crusty lips and cracked his knuckles. "And rule breakers must be punished."

25

THE TERRIBLE TRUTH

Bastien jumped back just in time to avoid Monsieur Xavier's sweeping, thrashing limbs. In the commotion, his reading light clattered to the floor.

Running was instinctual but it took several seconds for Bastien to spin on his heels and sprint away. Sami and Theo were already ahead. He tried to focus; one wrong turn and he would be lost for ever under the city. The faint light of Monsieur Xavier's torch did nothing to illuminate the tunnels ahead.

The smacking of footsteps on the ground behind them was as loud as a mining drill. Monsieur Xavier had firecrackers in the soles of his shoes and each step was an explosion.

"You can't outrun me!"

Bastien tried to ignore the director's screams, but they still sent a jolt of fear right through him. He ran faster, careful not to trip over his own feet. He followed the sound of Sami and Theo up ahead, their voices the only thing that could guide him through the pitch-black tunnels.

"You won't make it out of here!" Monsieur Xavier laughed.

The muscles in Bastien's legs grew tight and he ignored the pain in the soles of his feet, even though each step felt like walking over a bed of hot coals.

The ground underneath him rose up suddenly, and Bastien tripped, flying forward onto his stomach.

"Come on, Bastien!" Theo's voice cried from further down the tunnel.

Bastien scrambled onto his feet, his hands cut and dirty.

"Theo! Sami?"

No response came to his calls, only his own voice echoing back at him and the taunts of Monsieur Xavier. Now, Bastien had to feel his way along as he ran, his hands trailing against the rough walls.

He didn't notice the dead end until he ran straight

into the wall. The impact sent him flying and his face scraped against the rock.

Warm drops of blood trickled down Bastien's forehead. He kept his hand on his head and backed into a corner. If he had any chance of escape, he needed to be alert. Clinging to the shadows would buy him time.

The sound of approaching footsteps pounded in Bastien's ears and he squeezed his eyes shut.

"Come on out, Bastien. Why delay the inevitable?"

Bastien slowed his breathing. Where were Theo and Sami? He needed his friends.

"You're always sticking your nose where it doesn't belong." Monsieur Xavier's sigh filled the air. "Just like your parents."

The mention of his parents pulled Bastien out of the shadows. Monsieur Xavier was baiting him, daring him to ask the question that had plagued his thoughts. As certain as he was, he needed to hear it from Monsieur Xavier's mouth.

"You were there at the hotel, weren't you? You were in the room opposite. You started the fire and disappeared before the police could find you."

There was a hissing sound and light blinded Bastien. He scrambled to his feet. In front of him, Monsieur

Xavier stood with a flaming torch in his hand and a menacing look plastered on his face.

"No point lying about it now, I suppose. I made sure that the last view your parents ever had was of me and the flames on the other side of their hotel door." Monsieur Xavier took a step closer and Bastien saw the red lining of his cloak – the cloak he'd worn to kidnap writers in the dead of night. Had he been wearing it when he killed Bastien's parents too?

"Poor Margot and Hugo didn't stand a chance." Monsieur Xavier placed the torch on the ground and moved closer.

Bastien's grief hit him anew. It rose from the tips of his toes up to the hairs on his head, and then came crashing and spilling out. "How could you?"

"They discovered Olivier's cunning can't be contained. As will you."

Bastien flinched, his throat turning as dry as dust. "So Olivier Odieux ordered my parents' death."

Monsieur Xavier simply shrugged. "He didn't want them meddling in his business any longer."

"What was so important that it was worth taking my parents away from me? What did they know?"

A wicked grin tugged at Monsieur Xavier's lips.

"That notebook has proved quite an inconvenience, but not any more."

"You're not taking anything else from me. I'm leaving here alive." Bastien stood firm and mustered every drop of courage. "With my notebook."

"You're too late. It's already on its way to Olivier."

"You don't have it?" Bastien's panic pierced through his anger. It wasn't something to be passed around carelessly. Those pages contained his whole life: past, present and future.

"My other, useless but obedient, brother is delivering the notebook to Olivier as we speak. You're too late to find out the secrets it contains. You can't change anything."

"My parents didn't keep any secrets from me!"

Monsieur Xavier rolled his eyes. "What you believe and what you don't know are two very different things."

"I won't stop until you pay for what you did," Bastien said, ignoring his taunts. "Not just for my parents, but for every writer you've kidnapped." A lump caught in his throat. "You've taken so much away from all of us. You've made a misery of every boy's life in the orphanage. But it stops now."

"I can take what I want," Monsieur Xavier spat. "Haven't you learned by now?" His black hair clung to his cheeks, giving him the look of a wolf, wild and ravenous. He took a step forward, his hands outstretched. "And now I have your notebook, I can finally finish the Bonlivre job."

Monsieur Xavier pounced just as the ground beneath their feet groaned. There was a sharp shudder and a crack slowly split the passage floor in two. It grew wider and Bastien edged back, clinging to the wall for purchase.

A look of panic spread over Monsieur Xavier's face, like a badly fitting mask. But it quickly disappeared, replaced with one of calm menace.

"It's too late for such tricks to save you."

"It's not me!" The floor beneath them continued to split open, like an earthquake gaining strength.

With one long half-step, half-jump, Monsieur Xavier bounded forward and landed on Bastien's side of the gap. He lunged towards the boy and gripped him by the wrists.

"Let go!" Bastien thrashed fiercely, but he was no match for Monsieur Xavier's ironclad grip.

"*Tais-toi!* I prefer my victims to struggle in silence."

Monsieur Xavier's eyes gleamed with delight.

Bastien's vision flickered. He was losing strength, but there was a muffled cry and then two figures shot through the tunnel mouth. As though he'd willed them by the power of thought alone, Bastien saw his friends.

Theo rushed forward, stopping just short of the crack's edge. He picked up Monsieur Xavier's dropped torch and waved it.

"You have to jump!" Theo shouted.

"You can do it!" called Sami.

Bastien followed the light of the torch, which called to him like a beacon. His friends were here and they gave him a new strength. This wasn't how his story was going to end.

He pushed against Monsieur Xavier and they stumbled backwards together.

"I'm afraid Bastien *can't* do it," Monsieur Xavier snarled, his fingernails digging into Bastien's skin.

He lifted Bastien up by his wrists, his grip burning and deepening, and dangled him over the edge of the ever-widening crack.

Theo cried out as Sami held him back, but Bastien refused to give in to his fate. The tiny ember of fight that was left in him sparked anew and, with the anger of a thousand war cries, he swung his legs. His foot caught on the edge of the crack and he used that to launch himself forward, shoving into Monsieur Xavier. The man stumbled back, surprised by the force of the blow. He'd underestimated Bastien's courage: it could move mountains and bring grown men to their knees.

Free from the director's grip, Bastien braced himself to jump. It was the only option. He looked ahead at Theo and Sami, their arms outstretched. If he looked down at the abyss, his feet would grow roots. He took a step back, his eyes fixed on his friends. He could make it to them.

Bastien took a deep breath and launched himself as far as he could, willing himself to reach his friends' embrace.

Darkness and fear seemed to swallow him, but a moment later he landed, legs sprawled, on the other side. His head spun from the impact, and clouds of dust and dirt choked his lungs.

Theo and Sami pulled him to his feet and they edged away from the chasm that now lay between them and Monsieur Xavier.

"Let's stop these games, shall we?" All traces of

amusement were gone from Monsieur Xavier's voice. He paced at the edge, ready to jump.

"We need to go!" Theo shouted.

Then a sharp cry demanded their attention. Bastien turned to see Monsieur Xavier slip at the crack's edge. The ground moaned, hungry for an offering, and the director plummeted like a bird falling from the sky.

Bastien stepped forward to peer over the edge. Monsieur Xavier was holding on by the tips of his fingers, his cloak flapping wildly behind him. He looked at the man's pleading face and felt a pang of guilt. But such evil didn't deserve Bastien's pity.

Unexpectedly Sami jolted forward, and bent over the edge, pulling something from Monsieur Xavier's cloak pocket.

"Get off me!" the director wailed.

As quick as a finger snap, Sami ran back down the tunnel, something shiny in his hand. To Bastien, it looked like an obsessively polished coin.

"We need to go now!" Theo pulled Bastien further into the tunnel.

"You won't escape this," Monsieur Xavier cried.

Bastien glanced back for a last look.

Monsieur Xavier's face came as a shock.

He was smiling.

And then the ground swallowed him whole.

"What in the name of Notre-Dame just happened?"

Bastien had no answer for Theo. He dropped to his knees in utter exhaustion; glowing, yellow dots blurred his vision and his head pounded with the force of a thousand drums.

"That tunnel is booby-trapped," Sami said.

"Booby-trapped how?" Theo's eyes glinted, keen and attentive.

"For years, robbers and criminals have used the catacombs to help them break into buildings. They've dug and drilled their ways into banks and museums from underground," Sami explained. "Explorers, people who love and protect the catacombs and the city tunnels, have set traps all across the tunnels to stop them."

As Theo and Sami discussed traps of every kind, Bastien descended further into his haze. Escaping from his thoughts was like wading through a swamp in a great fog: impossible. Monsieur Xavier was the reason for his misery. The fire had been no accident.

"He confessed."

"What did you say?" Theo's head snapped in his direction.

"Monsieur Xavier told me he started the fire that killed my parents." It was no longer just a suspicion, but the truth of what had happened. To speak it out loud made Bastien's entire body wilt, and he heaved for air, his lungs heavy.

"I'm so sorry, Bastien." Theo set his jaw, his teeth grinding against his cheeks. "How can one man be the source of so much evil?"

"It was an order from Olivier. Apparently my parents knew something about his plans, but I never heard them mention his name."

"Maybe they just didn't want to worry you?" Theo said.

"We told each other everything!" Bastien's tears flooded. "We were The Three Musketeers." He thought of Monsieur Xavier's taunts, about his parents keeping secrets from him. Were they just the words of a bitter, twisted man? Or did they contain some truth?

"My heart is with you, Bastien." Sami spoke finally. "Nothing can ever take away the pain of losing a parent."

"Did he have your notebook?" Theo gently steered the conversation.

Bastien shook his head, blinking back more tears. "It's with his brother. He's taking it to Olivier in Montmartre."

"Monsieur Xavier has a brother?" Theo shuddered. "Just when I thought it couldn't get any worse."

"He said there were secrets in the notebook." Bastien wiped his eyes. "What if my parents left me a clue about Monsieur Xavier and Olivier, but I was too foolish to realize? What did I miss?"

"You are far from foolish." Theo kneeled beside him, the torch burning brightly in his grip. "Every other word that came out of Monsieur Xavier's mouth was a lie. It might not be true."

"Maybe," Bastien replied. "But the way Monsieur Xavier looked at me, how he talked to me about my parents. It didn't feel like a lie."

The obsession with his notebook made sense to Bastien now. His parents had left him something to find out and Monsieur Xavier had stolen that away from him too.

In the corner of his eye, he spotted a flash of metal in Sami's grip.

"Did you get it back? What Monsieur Xavier stole from you?"

"Yes." Sami nodded. "He had it on him, as I thought he would."

"What was it?"

At the question, Sami recoiled like a snail in its shell. "It doesn't matter." His voice was soft but his words snapped. He turned away and set off down an adjacent tunnel. "Come on! We're not far from Montmartre now."

The sting of a question left unanswered hurt Bastien. He'd thought Sami trusted them, but there was no time to consider that now. They had to press on; Montmartre awaited. Bastien had to get his notebook back before it reached Olivier. It was about more than just his story now. He had to discover what his parents had hidden in its pages.

He rose, still unsteady on his feet. Theo held out his arm and Bastien took it, grateful for the support. He was eager to leave behind the horror of the tunnels and Monsieur Xavier.

Bastien wished their paths would never cross again. But he knew the director was like a cat; he had more lives to live, and in each one he was destined to find Bastien.

26

TEARS ON THE TRACKS

"**W**e're not lost."

"We are absolutely *perdu*! I've just seen the same skull I saw ten minutes ago."

"How can you tell the difference?"

"This one has a splat-shaped hole where the nose should be." Bastien stopped in his tracks. "It looks like it did a massive sneeze in the afterlife." He poked the hole with his finger. "Face it, we're going round in circles, Sami. We can't afford to waste any more time. If we don't get back to the orphanage in time with proof then Alice will have convinced the police to come with her for nothing."

"I told you I know the way." Sami knew these tunnels best. The others had only read about them in books, which wasn't the same as living and breathing the damp, dusty air down here like he had.

He remembered the first time he'd entered the catacombs, one winter ago. He'd been sleeping at the Gare du Nord, on a metal bench just outside the station toilets, when a policeman had forced him onto the streets. Desperately seeking somewhere to keep warm, Sami had stumbled upon an entrance to the tunnels, a hole in a grate behind a wine cellar. He hadn't expected to find himself down here again, but life was a lot like the catacombs: unpredictable and often muddled.

"I said I'd take you to Montmartre. Would you rather go alone?"

"Definitely not." Theo looked at Bastien with pleading eyes. There was no time to argue.

Bastien shrugged in defeat. Every extra minute in the catacombs was a minute less to find Monsieur Xavier's brother. The watch he'd taken from the office, which was now dirty and chipped, was fast approaching five in the morning. Getting his notebook back felt like an impossible task, but the things that they had already done had also felt impossible.

"These tunnels are endless," Bastien said. "You've got what you wanted, but my notebook is still out there."

Sami flinched. "I haven't got what I want. Not even close."

The narrowing tunnel ahead forced them onto their hands and knees. Bastien's muscles ached as he clawed his hands into the ground, dirt seeping under his fingernails and staining his palms. Theo was behind him, holding the director's torch between his teeth; the space was too small to carry it aflame. In front of them both, Sami crawled quickly on all fours, grunts and moans escaping from his lips. Then, his grunts stopped completely and Bastien crawled forward, panic bubbling in his chest.

"Sami?" he called out, but no reply came. It was as though the boy had fallen from a cliff edge.

"What happened?" The narrow tunnel muffled Theo's voice.

"Sami's disappeared!" Bastien crawled faster, ignoring the knots of pain twisting his back. He put one hand in front of the other, his skin grazing against the sharp stones that covered the ground. But then, the ground fell away from under him and Bastien fell down a chute, twisting and turning like a slide. His throat closed up in fear before he could warn Theo.

The hole spat Bastien out like a burp, and he landed on the floor with a thud. He lay there for a moment, afraid to stand. Dizziness held a powerful charm over his body. He waited until the blood rushed back through his veins and slowly got up, one foot and then the other.

He was standing on an abandoned station platform. Light was seeping in from somewhere above and it bounced off the green and white tiles covering the walls. Rats, black as night, scurried along the track and a broken Métro carriage lay on its side further along the tracks, its doors rusted and flaking. Bastien squinted to read the faded sign: *Gare du Nord*. They'd made it to the old station tracks and now a stone's throw away from Montmartre. Sami had been leading them in the right direction, after all. He'd brought them even closer to the surface of the city.

A thud and a yelp behind Bastien announced Theo's arrival on the platform.

"I think my heart flew out of my mouth." Theo rubbed his head and grabbed the torch which had clattered onto the floor beside him. "Are you okay?"

"I think so." Bastien held an arm out to Theo and helped him to his feet.

Something rumbled in the distance. It grew louder and louder and the sound of a train rattled on the other side of the wall. Bastien walked over and placed his hand against the tiles, the small vibrations jolting through his senses.

"Sami! Where are you?" Theo called.

The loud clunk of a stone hitting the wall answered the call. They walked up the platform and found Sami sitting on top of the overturned train carriage. His legs dangled over the window and he wore a faraway look – a look Bastien knew all too well.

"Sami." Bastien sat down on the platform edge and Theo kneeled beside him. "Which way do we follow the tracks?"

Instead of answering, Sami took something from his pocket and pressed it to his chest, as though he wanted to meld it in the shape of his heart.

"You asked me what Monsieur Xavier stole from me." Sami opened his palm. "It was this."

Dangling from Sami's grip was a cross made of bronze and silver, hanging from a green and red striped ribbon, in the centre of which sat a bronze star. A few surface scratches ran through the middle of the star, but even they couldn't tarnish its beauty.

Bastien had never seen a Croix de Guerre before. His father had told him tales of bravery from the war, of the soldiers who had been given such military decorations for their efforts. The medal was the sign of a true hero.

"Yassine Afriat was the most courageous soldier there ever was," Sami finally spoke again. "This medal is all I have left of Baba. Monsieur Xavier took it from me the day I arrived at the orphanage. I feared he would sell it."

Bastien wasn't surprised that Monsieur Xavier had kept hold of it; some things were far too precious even for the most despicable of humans to part with.

"Yassine was your father?" Bastien asked quietly.

"Baba was a foot soldier recruited from Morocco and forced to fight for France in the war." Emotion choked Sami's throat but he wrestled out of its grip. "I didn't want him to go, but he had no choice."

Although Bastien felt the weight of Sami's words, he knew that he could never truly understand. The war had changed everything for everyone, but it had ripped some people's lives in half, beyond repair, especially the *tirailleurs*.

"He sent us letters, but he never mentioned the war. All he cared about was whether Immi was managing and whether we were helping around the house." Sami smiled; memories of his sister Leïla floated to the surface. He wondered how tall she was now.

"His letters stopped just before the war ended. We didn't know what had happened to him. Immi said that he would've wanted us to carry on, but I couldn't let go of the hope, no matter how small, that he was still alive. The years passed in silence and it was torture. So I left home last summer and came to France to look for him. I left a note for my family and told them I'd be back with Baba by my side."

"That was incredibly brave," Theo said.

Bastien's heart ached with sympathy for Sami. Everything about the day when he'd found Sami crying in the bathroom now made sense. His tears had been for what he'd been through, what he'd lost, and what he was so desperate to get back to.

"It was foolish." Sami gripped the medal tighter and the cross dug into his palm. "What sort of idiot believes they can find one person in a foreign country of millions? I can't imagine the hurt I've caused my family back home in Mogador."

"You're not foolish," Bastien said, thinking of his parents and how he'd have done anything to save them. "Did you find him?"

Sami sniffed. "No one wanted to help me at first. My saviour was a nurse in a hospice near the River Aisne. She told me a solider called Yassine had lived there for a year after the war, clinging onto life. Gas had poisoned his lungs and he could barely speak."

Sami fumbled with the clip and pinned the medal to his jacket.

"But when he finally spoke, Baba told her to hold onto the medal until his only son came to claim it. He knew I would come looking for him – I was always just as headstrong as him."

Tears raced down Sami's cheeks but he held his head high.

"He passed away before I reached him. I would've given anything to have seen him again, one last time. The nurse gave me the cross and what money she could spare. I planned to hide on a train to Marseille, but the police caught me at the station and brought me to the orphanage."

Sami threw a handful of stones onto the track below. There was nothing Bastien could say to ease Sami's suffering. Like all the boys, he'd carried it around with him for such a long time, he'd grown used to its back-breaking strength.

Still, Bastien felt compelled to say something. Where normal words failed, stories always succeeded.

"Would you allow me to tell you a tale?" Bastien asked.

Sami nodded gently. "A distraction would be nice."

Then Bastien began.

"A fierce determination pumped through Sami's veins. It was this determination that forced him across the Mediterranean Sea in search of his father.

"His mother and sister would wake that morning and find his bed empty. Under his pillow was a message: that he had gone to France to find their father and that he'd be back one day. It was a promise he intended to keep.

"Sami's life completely changed when he found himself in a strange country, with the knowledge that his father had died and no money to pay for his passage home. He'd discovered his father had been the bravest of the brave; a lion on the battlefield.

"Sami had always known his father had been a hero, but the bronze medal that the nurse gave him, the last of his father's possessions, confirmed it to the world. Sami wore his father's Croix de Guerre each day and it gave him the courage to find his way back home.

"When the last train from Gare de Lyon rolled out of the platform, Sami went with it too.

"He slipped into the toilet cubicle, fastening the lock behind him. Huddled on the toilet lid, and praying no one would come knocking on the door, Sami stared out of the window.

"Crowded cities soon gave way to rolling countryside and terracotta buildings. Sami marvelled at the Roman amphitheatre ruins as the train rolled past Nîmes and then Montpellier, cities he'd only ever heard about. Finally he arrived in the port of Sète, and fled from the train before anyone noticed he wasn't supposed to be there.

"Bravery and cunning and a dash of undistilled luck led Sami onto the steamship. A sleeping security officer allowed him to slip past unnoticed and he nestled between two wooden crates full of rice. Closing his eyes, he dreamed of home, which was creeping closer with every wave.

"After what felt like hours, Sami woke to the sound of a commotion; of market sellers and calls to prayer. He snuck up onto the deck where the palm-fringed port of Tangier came into view. Sami became so restless he almost threw himself overboard.

"Disembarking at Tangier, he was prepared to walk the distance that would lead him home to Mogador. He passed the line of taxi cars outside the port, ignoring the calls of the drivers all haggling with each other to offer a better price.

"One man, tall and burly, with a smile like melted butter, stopped in front of Sami.

"'I'll take you wherever you need to go, free of charge,' the man said, admiring the medal pinned to his shirt. 'No distance is too far for the son of a selfless man.'

"When the city walls of his home appeared on the horizon, Sami stifled a cry. The man dropped him at the harbour and Sami, too impatient, broke into a sprint, running until his legs lost all feeling.

"His mother and sister opened the door and welcomed him home with open arms and faces wet with tears. All of their love and worry that had been bottled up ever since he left came spilling out in that one hug. They swept him inside and he told them everything.

"His mother sank to her knees and clutched the medal in her hands tenderly, like she was cradling her husband. The pain of losing her love would never leave, but she had her son back, and the hole that had appeared in her heart years ago began to slowly heal itself.

"When Sami kissed them goodnight, he placed his father's medal under his pillow and there it would stay, always.

"The people who love you never give up.

"And the people who care about you will never let you give up hope."

Sami's sobs grew quieter and he looked down at Bastien.

"I only hope my story has the same ending."

253

"I can't imagine how difficult it has been for you. Grief is a stream that ebbs and flows. Some days, it's calm and laps at your feet. But on bad days, it rises up like a tidal wave and pulls you underwater."

"That's exactly how I feel," Sami admitted quietly. "I've just never been able to find the words."

"You're in luck." Theo smiled, his arms tucked under his legs. "Words are Bastien's speciality."

Bastien stood up and jumped down onto the tracks below. He landed with a thud and rats scurried off in different directions. Sami wiped his eyes and lowered himself down from the carriage roof. Theo removed the last match from his pocket and relit the torch, its amber glow lighting up a fraction of the tunnels ahead.

"Just know that whenever you find the right words, we're here to listen," Bastien said.

Each of them had a story sad enough to fill an ocean with tears. It was remarkable, Sami's strength to weather such a hurricane.

"I appreciate it." Sami nodded. "Come, we must take the north tunnel."

Bastien promised himself, as they followed the tracks into the tunnel mouth, that Sami would get the hero's ending that he deserved.

After another hour of zigzagging through tunnels, the marking on the arch in front of them was a sight for sore eyes.

"We're under Boulevard de la Chapelle." Sami grinned. "We'll be in Montmartre in no time."

Bastien and Theo walked as quickly as marching-band leaders, sticking to Sami's shadow as he navigated the endless tunnel bends.

Bastien was desperate to see Paris above ground and he made a promise to himself to never take the beauty of the city for granted as long as he lived. It dawned on him that he hadn't been this far north since the day he was sent to the orphanage. The apartment he'd once called home was now home to someone else, a thought which left a funny taste in his mouth.

"When we get your notebook back and your story sells for thousands of francs, where shall we live?" Theo asked, noticing the faraway look on Bastien's face. "How about the Palace of Versailles?" Theo's optimism was catching and Bastien found himself smiling again.

"Think about how enormous the library would be." Bastien dreamed of the beautiful books that would line the ceiling-high shelves. "What about you, Sami?"

Sami found it almost impossible to be optimistic when life had, so far, always taught him to expect the worst. Dreams were made to be clutched tightly to your chest and shared with nobody. Otherwise, they'd never come true.

"There's got to be something you'd wish for?" Theo asked.

Sami's dream poked at him and so he finally said it out loud.

"Your story was my dream. I want to go back to Mogador where I can see the ocean from my bedroom window. I want to hug my family and sit around, laughing while we eat my favourite dinner, a potato and green olive tagine. I want to walk along the beach and watch the sun set." Sami sighed. "That is all I want."

Sami paused, allowing himself to bask in his dream a moment longer, then he turned away, not wanting them to see the quiver of his bottom lip.

They continued to cut through the darkness as cleanly as a scythe. The tunnel soon led to a disused sewage pipe and, as they crawled through it on their stomachs, Bastien wished he had a third hand to pinch his nose. The air was pungent and he was glad when his feet touched rocky ground again.

"There should be a hatch somewhere nearby," Sami said. "There's one in every neighbourhood that will lead us back up to the city."

Bastien had been underground for too long and it was beginning to seep into his mind when he smelled something…something different. The heavy dampness had lifted; what he could smell now was fresh air, the type that filled crisp morning skies. It was the type of air that Bastien was desperate to fill his lungs with.

"We must be close," Bastien shouted and walked quicker, a spring in his step. "I can smell the city!" His notebook was somewhere in Montmartre, right above him. There was still so much more that they needed to do to make everything right. They had to take proof of Monsieur Xavier's guilt back to the orphanage and to the police, who would help free the missing writers. And he needed to get his notebook back and find out what his parents had known about Olivier. It was overwhelming.

At the end of the tunnel, a rickety wooden ladder rose upwards. Bastien raced towards the ladder and climbed as quickly as he could. It led to a wooden hatch just as Sami had described. There it was: their gateway back to Paris that would illuminate his path through Montmartre to his notebook. The path would also lead him straight to Olivier, but as much as that frightened Bastien, he needed answers more than ever.

Bastien pushed against the hatch. It groaned and lifted slightly, but then snapped back down. He tried again and again, but with no luck.

He refused to be beaten. Paris was full of old things – a city of dusty relics and buried treasures, just waiting to be found and serve a purpose. They'd found the hatch and now it was meant to free them. Bastien believed this with all his being.

"Here, let me try!" Theo climbed up the ladder and squeezed past Bastien. His fingers poked Bastien in the eye as Theo passed the torch to him to hold.

Unsurprisingly, Theo's attempt was no better. The

hatch creaked, as though laughing at their efforts.

On the other side of the hatch was freedom. Freedom for him, Sami and Theo. Freedom for the rest of the boys at the orphanage. Alice would soon wake and set her side of their plan into motion. She expected him to meet her at the orphanage with evidence of Monsieur Xavier's guilt at eight o'clock. Time was running out.

Bastien would force this hatch open even if his shoulder shattered into a million pieces.

"It will open if we all push together!" The ladder swayed with the added weight of Sami. They moved carefully; one wrong move could break the rungs and send them tumbling back down.

Bastien felt every muscle in his body stretch in perfect harmony, ready to push one more time.

"Poussons!" Bastien cried.

The hatch swung open. It took a moment for Bastien to realize the cries of delight he heard were his own.

He pulled himself up and out and breathed in the fresh air. It was still dark outside, a faint pre-dawn glow creeping across the sky, but in comparison to the tunnels, it felt like a bright summer's day.

Bastien rubbed his eyes and looked up, immediately realizing where he was; the white stone of the Sacré-

Cœur couldn't be mistaken. They'd crawled out of the tunnels at the very bottom of the church steps.

"We made it!" Bastien cried. "We're in Montmartre."

Theo shot past him, followed closely by Sami. They ran up and down the street, yelling and laughing.

"I'll never take you for granted again." Theo dropped down onto his knees and tried to hug the pavement. "I promise you, oh lovely solid floor, I'll never leave you."

A smile, dripping with relief, appeared on Bastien's face. They were finally free of the tunnels.

The streets of Montmartre were still deserted, as morning had not yet properly arrived. Bastien checked the watch. It was just after seven o'clock, only one hour until Alice returned to the orphanage. The tunnels below had been a black hole, sucking any concept of time from them. They needed to hurry.

But turning to face Sami, Bastien was taken aback. Where he'd been so joyous only a moment ago, he now looked at Bastien and Theo with sad eyes.

"What's the matter?"

"This is it," Sami said. He stuck out his hand and it took Bastien a moment to realize he was saying goodbye. "This is where I leave you."

On the bottom steps of the Sacré-Cœur, Bastien wrestled with the sinking feeling in the pit of his stomach. Sami had his father's medal back, that had been his plan all along. But now that they were here in Montmartre, Bastien couldn't imagine carrying on without the three of them together.

Sami looked down at the ground. He'd promised to take Bastien and Theo to Montmartre and he'd kept his word. What else was here for him? He had an ocean to cross.

"I wish you luck, Bastien," Sami continued. "No one should be without the last memory of their parents."

Bastien swept Sami into a tight hug. It took Sami

by surprise, for he couldn't remember the last time someone had hugged him. It felt good.

They broke apart and Sami nodded solemnly at Theo. It didn't stop the smaller boy running forward and hugging Sami tightly too.

"We'll miss you," Theo said.

"I'll miss you both too." The words barely emerged from Sami's mouth, and with a wave, he set off down the sloping street.

Bastien's heart flew to his throat. He couldn't watch his new friend walk away.

"Wait!" he cried. "Don't go just yet. I can't do this without you." He looked at Theo's equally crestfallen face. "*We* can't do this without you."

Sami had navigated them through the catacombs and, with him by their side, they'd been stronger than they'd ever thought possible.

"We still need to find Monsieur Xavier's brother and get my notebook back. If he's taking it to Olivier's house, then we have to outnumber them," Bastien continued. "We need our third musketeer."

Sami stopped in his tracks. In front of him, Paris loomed large; the city that had chewed him up and swallowed him whole. He had to get back home to his family – that was the thought that had helped him through the bleakest of times. But now he had Bastien and Theo, two true friends. Could he leave them to finish alone what they'd started together?

"When it's over, and we've freed the writers, I promise you this: I will help you find your way home," Bastien called as he ran towards him. "You said no one can promise you that, but I mean it. Whatever it takes, you'll return home and walk along the beach with your family again."

A moment's pause stretched into an eternity of uncertainty.

"I suppose", Sami turned around, his voice calm, "that I cannot refuse friends." He walked back up the pavement and held out his hand. "I will hold you to your word, Bastien, and you can hold me to mine: I will help you finish this."

Great heroes always had great plans and Bastien had read about many of them, but now he needed one of his own. Unlike in fairy tales and myths, he couldn't battle the unnatural wonders of the world alone. A great plan required the help of even greater friends who were cunning, quick-witted and brave. Luckily for Bastien,

Theo and Sami possessed all these qualities and more.

"We need to get into Olivier's house undetected," Sami said. They sat, huddled, on the bottom church step. "What was the address again?"

"13, Rue de la Bonne." Bastien thought of the letters in Monsieur Xavier's office. If the director had been working with Olivier all this time, then those letters were more proof of their scheming.

"Lucky number 13," Sami muttered.

"Luckily for us, I still have my lockpick," Theo said, his hands already fidgeting in his pockets.

"Do you think that will work?" Bastien asked. He suspected Olivier Odieux's house was a fortress. So many stolen words had made Olivier as rich as a king and he wouldn't be giving anything up without a fight.

Theo shrugged. "It will have to be. You're not doubting my skills now, are you?"

"Of course not. If anyone can do it, it's you. Theo the Talented!"

Breaking into Olivier's house was a risky plan, Bastien knew that much, but they'd already done a lot of risky, impossible things. One more couldn't possibly hurt, could it?

Louis stood outside Olivier's house, his trousers dripping wet and ripped. Xavier's shortcut had been anything but short. It had sent him down into the darkest depths of the catacombs and he'd almost lost his mind. He'd squeezed through gaps, danced around stalagmites, and waded through several flooded tunnels. All in the name of family.

Louis had lost more hours than he cared to count, but now the terrible journey was behind him and he was here. He fished the notebook from his coat pocket and held it in his hands. All that was left was to pass it over to Olivier. The instructions were perfectly clear…but now there was hesitation in his mind and the soles of his feet.

Something had changed. And that something was Louis.

The small notebook weighed heavily in his pocket as he turned the key in the lock. The door creaked open and Louis shuffled wearily down the hallway. Every bone in his body groaned with the effort of keeping him upright. He crept past the sitting room, ignoring the life-size sculpture of Olivier. It had always scared him.

The steps of the horseshoe staircase squeaked and Louis cursed under his breath. This house wasn't on his side; it wanted him to make noise and anger Olivier. He glanced up at the stairs twirling high above; eighty-eight steps were all that separated him and the notebook from Olivier.

When he handed it over, that would be it. He was going to tell Olivier goodbye and leave the family business for good.

Louis reached the first-floor landing and tiredness hit him like a boxer's punch. He hadn't slept in over twenty-four hours; the tunnels had robbed him of any rest. Now every step felt like wading in cement. The door to one of the many guest bedrooms was ajar and Louis hesitated. He'd made it here in one piece with the notebook. He could afford a few minutes to catch his breath, couldn't he?

Bastien climbed the Sacré-Cœur steps, tripping over his feet in anticipation. The view at the top of Montmartre was always a sight to marvel at. Even in the hazy glow of early dawn, he could see the flashing lights of Pigalle, the frosty rooftops stacked next to each other like dominoes, and the curving spine of the river Seine as it wove itself delicately through the city centre like a single thread through a needle eye. His city provided endless inspiration and this view reminded him of evenings with his parents on their apartment balcony.

Olivier had taken that all away, but he wasn't going to take Bastien's notebook. It was the last piece of his parents and he was determined to get it back.

"Rue de la Bonne is a little further down here," Sami called. Bastien turned away from the view and followed him and Theo deeper into the sloping streets of Montmartre.

"How do you know the area so well?" Theo asked. "You're a walking map of the city!"

"I've stayed in many places throughout Paris. There's a garden square at the bottom of this road where I used to sleep sometimes. It was a good place to look at the stars."

Bastien swallowed down a sympathetic smile. Sami didn't need it.

"When you return to Mogador, you'll sleep for a thousand nights in your own bed."

"I hope you're right." Sami smiled at Bastien. "The street is on the left here."

They turned left into Rue de la Bonne, a steep and wide tree-lined street full of grand houses and apartment buildings. Bastien counted the door numbers as they walked, taking in the majesty of each house. How much had Olivier stolen to live on a street like this?

"Here we are, number 13!" Theo pointed to a grand gate surrounded by tall oak trees. A chimney peeped over the top of the branches but the rest of the house was completely hidden.

"Try to stay in the shadow of the trees." Checking the street was empty, Bastien climbed the gate with ease, Sami and Theo right beside him. They lowered themselves down into a thicket of trees on the other side. Bastien pushed back a branch and saw a house fit for a king. He stared at the four storeys stacked on top of each other like a wedding cake. The stained-glass windows were decorated with white and gold shutters, and the balconies were large enough to hold half of Paris.

Two pillars, carved into the shape of pens, stood on either side of an arched doorway. A vast oak door, painted blood-red, loomed large.

"So this is where all the wealthy in the city live." Theo's face twisted. "How can Olivier have so much when so many Parisians go hungry each day?" He walked over to the water fountain in the front garden, which was the shape of an inkpot and sculpted in marble.

"This house was built on the work of other writers," Bastien said. "He doesn't deserve a single brick of it."

High up, a single light shone from a small attic window. Was Monsieur Xavier's brother already inside? Had he delivered the notebook to Olivier? Bastien readied himself. Despite its luxurious appearance, he knew that this house would hold horrors inside. "Ready? We're not leaving until we find my notebook."

Sami nodded.

"As ready as I'll ever be." Theo stepped forward, brandishing the lockpick in his hand like a weapon. While he worked, Sami kept watch on the street from the trees and Bastien gazed up at the house. A shadow flickered behind the attic window. Was someone up there?

Theo turned back to them, the door behind him ajar.

"Bravo, Theo," Bastien said. "That was quick!"

Theo smiled nervously. "It wasn't me. The door was already open."

The open door felt like an invitation, or a trap. With no other choice, Bastien stepped into Olivier Odieux's house and hoped he'd make it out again alive.

"Who would leave a door open to a house like this?" Sami whispered.

"Maybe Monsieur Xavier's brother is already here," Bastien replied. "He could've been in a rush."

A grotesque richness dripped from every corner of the house. Chandeliers hung from the ceiling and enormous crystal vases of red roses balanced on glass cabinets. Dozens of portraits lined the hallway and Bastien finally saw the face of Olivier Odieux, the man who had ordered his parents' death. Olivier looked like an unremarkable man, incapable of the crimes Bastien knew he'd committed. No longer was Bastien scared; he felt only anger.

"Bastien," Theo whispered. "Come look at this."

He slipped through a door and found Theo in the

front room of the house. He tiptoed past a marble sculpture of Olivier and walked over to where Theo was standing in front of a glass cabinet. It was full of trophies, awards and photographs from decadent parties.

"Reckon he's his own favourite person?" Theo smirked.

"All of his success is a lie." Bastien wanted to push the cabinet to the floor and watch it shatter into a thousand pieces. He wanted to break everything that mattered most to Olivier. He swallowed down his anger and rummaged through the room, overturning velvet cushions and rifling through cabinet drawers. But there was nothing. The notebook was nowhere to be seen.

"No luck in the dining room." Sami's head popped around the door. "Nothing in the kitchen either. The staircase is this way."

Bastien and Theo followed Sami down the hallway and into a large room. A gigantic horseshoe staircase twirled upwards to the full height of the house. Lit up by a sparkling chandelier, the staircase bathed in its own grandeur.

"It looks like it's been lifted straight from the Palace of Fontainebleau." Theo gawked.

Bastien raced up the steps, feeling each second slip

away from him. Olivier's house was huge. Would they have time to look through every room for his notebook if they were to get back to the orphanage to meet Alice and the police at eight as planned?

At the top of the stairs, a sound stopped him in his tracks. It was coming from behind a door at the end of the first-floor landing. He turned to Theo and Sami, a finger on his lips, and beckoned them to follow.

"Is that…someone snoring?" Sami frowned.

Bastien gave the door a gentle nudge. Through the crack he spied a lavish bedroom; red and gold painted walls and red drapes framing the balcony door. In the middle of the room was a palatial four-poster bed, and in it was a man, fast asleep, his hands clutched to his chest. His clothes looked dirty and wet and there was a large rip across the front of his coat.

"Is it Olivier?" Theo strained to look through the gap.

"I can't be sure." Bastien nudged the door further open. "I need to get closer."

"Go with him," Sami told Theo. "I'll keep guard on the landing."

They snuck through the gap and across the bedroom, the drapes swaying from the cold air coming through the half-open balcony door. A thin strip of light streamed in and lit up the man's face.

"It's Monsieur Xavier's brother!" Bastien was certain; the family likeness was strong.

He crept closer, Theo right behind him, up to the side of the bed, his eyes locking on the small square in the man's hands.

"He's got it! My notebook!" Bastien launched forward but Theo pulled him back.

"I'll get it," Theo said, peering over the edge of the bed. "I've got steadier hands than you."

"Be careful! We can't wake him."

Theo slipped his hand under the man's arm and pulled the corner of the notebook. Slowly, it inched away from his grip.

"One more second." Theo wriggled the notebook closer. He almost had both hands around it when the man sat up as straight as though he'd woken from a coffin.

Theo dropped the notebook on the bed and stumbled into Bastien. Both of them fell to the ground.

"Bastien Bonlivre." The man's voice wasn't aggressive, but full of sorrow. Bastien scrambled to his feet at the same time as the man got up. He stood slowly like he was made of papier-mâché and might fall apart at any moment. "The night has been so long, I just wanted a moment's rest," the man mumbled. "Olivier is waiting for me to bring him the notebook."

"Please..." Bastien couldn't hold back the desperation in his voice. It washed out of him. "Give it back."

But the man simply shook his head. "My brothers will kill me if I do."

"Brothers?" The realization made Bastien's skin crawl. "Olivier is your brother too?"

The man did an awkward half-bow. "I am Louis Odieux, the oldest of the Odieux brothers."

Bastien looked curiously at Louis. He didn't seem dangerous. If he had the same blood flowing through his veins, then he had to be. But, there was something in his eyes that Bastien had never seen in the director's before: compassion.

"Monsieur Xavier came to the orphanage because of me, didn't he? He followed me there right after the fire."

Louis sighed and swayed unsteadily on his feet. He ran one hand over his bare head and sat back down on the bed. "He did. Olivier thought Xavier would be able to find the notebook and destroy it. But you, Bastien, well you've proved to be more resourceful than most adults."

Bastien chanced another question, the one that had taunted him since Monsieur Xavier had first told him in the catacombs. "What is the secret in the notebook that they killed my parents for?"

"My brothers believe that your parents left information for you about Olivier's grand plan," admitted Louis.

"What information?" Bastien clenched his fists. "What grand plan?"

"I don't know," Louis whimpered.

"Tell Bastien the truth!" Theo kicked the bed.

"Honestly, they've schemed behind my back for so long. I don't know what your parents knew, but I can promise you this: whatever it was, whatever it is that they left for you to discover, it has Olivier worried beyond belief."

Bastien frowned. "How do you expect me to believe you?"

"I'm here, aren't I?" Louis said. "I could've raced up these stairs and delivered the notebook to Olivier straight away, but I didn't. My brothers' crimes have spiralled out of control."

"But you've stood by and watched them both hurt so many people." With Sami guarding the door outside, Bastien felt safe to ask Louis the questions running through his mind. "If you didn't agree with them, why didn't you go to the police? You could've stopped this all!"

"The line between good and bad is a thin one," Louis cowered, brushing a small spider from the hole on his jacket sleeve. "As you get older, it begins to blur."

"I disagree." Courage amplified Bastien's voice. "It's not blurred, but a solid line. It's indecision between good or bad that leads to the choices you make. You can make the choice to be good right now. My parents will have died for nothing if Olivier isn't stopped. What about the writers in the catacombs? Will you let them die in vain too?"

Louis had come to realize that his silence was almost as bad as starting the hotel fire himself. He'd stood by and let Xavier and Olivier spread so much evil. "You're right," he muttered. "I need to be brave. Like you."

"I haven't always been brave." Bastien glanced at Theo right beside him, poised and ready to defend his friend. "I needed help too."

"No longer shall I live in the shadows. Please, take back what's rightfully yours."

Louis held out the notebook and, with shaking hands, Bastien took it. He clutched it to his chest and the joy he felt only confirmed what he already knew; he would have gone to any lengths to get his notebook back. It meant the world to him.

"You have the right to uncover the secrets it holds. The world deserves to know what your parents discovered." Louis placed a hand on Bastien's shoulder. "One day, I hope you can forgive me for what I lacked the courage to do."

"My mother always said that holding a grudge is as pointless as a writer waiting for inspiration to strike." Bastien slipped his notebook into the secret pocket in his trouser lining.

Louis let out a sad laugh. "Your mother was incredibly wise. And so are you."

"I hate to interrupt," Theo interjected, "but now is probably a good time for us to get going."

"Your friend is right," Louis said. "Come, let's leave this place before we disturb the beast that is my brother. I know his routine. He will wake soon."

Bastien had had enough of beastly villains and they

needed to get back to the orphanage in time to meet Alice and show all the evidence they'd found to the police. But there was a part of him that wanted to stay, a part that wanted to march up the stairs and confront Olivier.

Then he thought of the writers in the catacombs and how every second they spent down there was a second too long. The sooner they got back, the sooner Sami could lead the police straight to the writers, sealing Monsieur Xavier and Olivier's fate.

For now, the secrets in his notebook would have to wait.

Outside on the landing, Sami was leaning against the staircase bannister. His eyes lingered on Louis as they all emerged from the bedroom. "Everything okay?"

"I've got it." Bastien patted his pocket. "Let's get out of here. We have to get back. Alice will be waiting with people who can help us."

"Okay, let's go." Sami's eyes darted up and down the staircase. "I haven't heard anything suspicious, but this whole house smells of danger."

"You have no idea," Louis muttered.

They walked back down the stairs and through the hallway. Bastien stole a glance at the last painting hanging on the wall. Olivier's face stared back at him, as unreadable as a hieroglyphic. Who really was this man who had destroyed his entire world?

"We have a problem." Theo said. "The door won't open."

"What do you mean?" A familiar feeling of panic rose in Bastien's chest. "It was open when we arrived!"

"Sometimes it jams." Louis stepped forward and fished a key out of his trench coat pocket. "It's an old building." He turned the key in the lock but there was no reassuring click. He tried again but the door remained firmly shut. Theo tried, this time with his lockpick in hand. Nothing worked.

"It's not going to open, is it?" Bastien knew the door wasn't jammed. Olivier was already awake and had sealed their exit, trapping them in his house like a tomb. Bastien's eyes darted around the hallway, sensing Olivier's presence as though he was breathing down his neck. "Is there another way out of here?"

Louis reached for his handkerchief and dabbed his forehead, which was now sweating profusely. He glanced about, his pupils restless and flitting. "There's a passageway in the cellar, but I'm not sure where it leads. I saw Olivier go down there one evening and he didn't come back up the same way, so it has to go somewhere."

"It's better than just waiting here," Bastien replied. "Let's go!"

Bastien, Theo and Sami followed Louis back into the grand hall, the staircase towering above them. Louis's eyes shot upwards, as he scurried across the hall and opened a small wooden door tucked behind the staircase. "Through here."

Creak.

Bastien froze mid-step.

"Come on, Bastien," Theo hissed. Louis and Sami had already disappeared through the door.

Creak.

The sound came again, followed by a blood-curdling laugh.

Bastien could hear Theo's shouts, begging him to move, but they passed right through him. The sound of footsteps on the staircase had hypnotized him.

Bastien knew who it was.

It was the man responsible for his parents' deaths.

Olivier Odieux had trapped them inside and now he was coming after Bastien.

30

THE BAD BROTHERS

Theo pulled him down into the cellar with such force, Bastien heard the *pop* of his joints. Their feet clattered against the stone steps; it was no use being quiet now.

The stairs opened onto a long, thin passageway, heavy wooden doors to the left and right. The closest door on the right was open, the sound of Sami's muttering coming from inside. Bastien stepped into a wine cellar, shelves upon shelves of wine bottles and large oak barrels covering the floor. The candles on the wall created a dim light, in which Bastien and Theo made out the figures of Louis and Sami at the end of the room.

"It was meant to be here, it must be here." Louis

pulled on a cupboard door handle, bottles smashing to the ground.

"What's wrong?"

"He's led us to a dead end." Sami stared furiously at Louis. "You've trapped us. You're still working for your brothers!"

"I promise I'm not." Louis held his hands up. "Please, you must believe me. I swear there was an exit down here. I wouldn't betray you, not now."

"My pathetic brother is telling you the truth," said a booming, clear voice. Bastien turned around and there he was: Olivier Odieux stood at the bottom of the cellar steps, his broad body covered in a red silk dressing gown. The man who'd ruined his life had just casually rolled out of bed.

"Brother, have mercy." Louis clasped his hands together.

"This house was built many years ago and contained a secret passageway leading to the Sacré-Cœur." Olivier ignored Louis and walked towards them, his velvet-slippered feet moving quietly across the floor. "I had a feeling that my brother would betray us and so I blocked the exit. I hoped, of course, that I was wrong, but it appears that family doesn't mean much to him."

"Family doesn't mean anything to you either!" Fury cut through Bastien's words. "You killed my parents!"

Olivier stopped just in front of them and looked Bastien up and down.

"Ah yes, Bastien. What an honour it is to finally meet Margot and Hugo's son. We have much to talk about."

"Don't speak their names!" Olivier's mocking enraged Bastien. How dare the man act so calm? How dare he smile at him!

"I can say what I like." Olivier shrugged. "After all, words are my weapon." He walked over to Louis and picked him up by the scruff of his coat collar. "And you, brother, you will pay."

"It was time to do the right thing." Louis's voice trembled. "Let the children go. They've done nothing to you."

"You jeopardized my plan in order to *do the right thing*?" Olivier spat out each word and dropped Louis on the floor. "You always were a spineless weakling."

"You're wrong." Louis pulled himself up. "I'll no longer sit by and watch you and Xavier spread your evil."

Olivier laughed. "Evil? I'm simply restoring the natural order of things." He turned to Bastien, his palms upturned and a sneer lingering on his lips. "I'm afraid

I'll need to take that notebook back from you."

"Not a chance." Bastien touched his pocket and, instinctively, Theo and Sami stood in front of him.

Olivier snarled. "How heart-warming to see you have such good friends. Three disgusting children for the price of one is an offer I can't refuse."

"You're outnumbered." Sami's voice didn't falter.

"He's right," Theo added. "You've got no choice but to let us go."

"That's where you're wrong." Olivier whistled and something clattered on the stairs. Footsteps slapped on the stone slab floor and a figure emerged in the doorway. Dragging himself towards them, his face bruised, his cloak tattered and wet, stood Monsieur Xavier with a broad grin on his face.

"Nice to see you again, boys."

Bastien stared at the director in disbelief. How had he survived the fall? The director was like a flea; impossible to get rid of.

"Did you really think you could dispose of me that easily?" Monsieur Xavier laughed. "I've survived more than my fair share of catacomb traps." He spat at Louis's feet. "And you are a disgrace."

"You won't get away with any of this!" Bastien looked

at Olivier and Monsieur Xavier, their mouths curled upwards with cruel smirks. "There are people who'll come looking for us, and for the writers too."

Olivier's eyes widened in amusement. "I doubt that. There are holes so deep underneath this city, ones only I know about. No one will find you for centuries. By then, of course, you'll be nothing more than bone dust."

"Why are you doing this?" The bottles on the shelves shook, such was the power of Bastien's voice.

"Why? Well, I suppose it's about time you and I had a chat, don't you think?" Olivier clapped his hands and Xavier turned to him.

"What orders, brother?"

"Take these two to the oubliette." Olivier waved his hand at Theo and Sami and, as quick as a cat, Xavier's hands were on both of their shoulders, pulling them back towards the stairs. "And, Louis, if you don't want Xavier to drop them both off the first-floor balcony, I suggest you follow closely behind."

"Let them go!" Bastien shouted. "This is between me and you!" It was all his fault. He'd led them on this journey to get his notebook back and now Theo and Sami were going to pay the price. The oubliette was a fate even worse than the Isolation Chamber. It was a dungeon at the bottom of a tiny, vertical shaft; Bastien had only ever read about them in history books about medieval times, but it was unsurprising that Olivier would have one in his own house. "Please," he begged. "Don't hurt them."

Bastien could only watch as Theo and Sami disappeared through the door, still thrashing in Monsieur Xavier's grip, followed by a trembling Louis.

Olivier turned to him and pointed his manicured finger. "Come along, Bastien. We have much to discuss."

31
THE LAST BONLIVRE

Bastien felt Olivier's eyes burning a hole in the back of his head with every step. They'd climbed two flights of stairs and now, as the last steps leading to the attic narrowed, Bastien wished for a never-ending staircase to save him from what lay ahead.

"*Vite*," Olivier instructed, poking him in the back.

Bastien shuddered and quickened his pace. How had everything gone wrong so quickly? He'd got his notebook back and they had been so close to escaping and getting back to the orphanage. The ornate clock on the staircase wall read half past eight. Would Alice realize something had gone wrong? He'd never broken a promise to her before. But how could she help them now if she didn't know where they were?

The small landing at the top of the stairs led to a single, red door. Bastien hesitated. If he walked through this door, he feared he'd never leave.

"Don't be scared." Olivier nudged him forward. "We'll have a nice little chat before I decide your fate."

The study was beautiful. Even in a state of fear, Bastien couldn't help but gaze at the mahogany bookcases and their sliding brass ladder. An unlit fireplace nestled in the chimney breast and a large marble desk sat under the window. The wide attic window looked out onto the whole of Montmartre and the city beyond. The view taunted him.

"There." Olivier pointed to the green leather chair in front of the desk. Bastien slumped down and pulled his knees up to his chest.

Olivier opened the top desk drawer and produced a coil of red rope, which he tied around Bastien's arms and ankles. "I'll be taking this as well." He pulled the notebook from Bastien's pocket lining in one swift movement.

"Whatever you think is in there, you're wrong." Bastien squirmed. "Don't destroy it."

"I can't recall ever being wrong." Olivier squeezed the notebook as though he was trying to wring the words from each page. "And haven't you learned that I can do whatever I want?" He walked over to the unlit fireplace and threw the notebook onto the middle of the wood pile. "Destroying this notebook is a necessary means to continue my plan. It's a problem. Just like your parents were."

Problem. The word hit Bastien so hard it winded him. He couldn't let Olivier light that fire; he had to keep him talking. "They did nothing to you!"

"They were always trying to be such good people." Olivier said the word *good* as though it was poisonous. "Your father thought he could change me."

Bastien frowned. He couldn't recognize his fiercely kind father as the type of person to be friends with such a devious man. "My father never mentioned you."

"This was long before you entered the world." Olivier's eyes glinted. "Your father lived a whole other life to the one you knew." Bastien noticed a fond smile pass across the man's face. "We had the world at our feet: two young men with bright eyes and even brighter ideas! That is, until he betrayed me. Typical Hugo – even from the grave, he's still trying to ruin me."

"You're lying!" Bastien couldn't picture his father standing in the same room as Olivier. Even with an imagination as big as his, it was impossible to fit them together.

Calmly, Olivier walked over to a bookcase. He picked up a photo frame and shook out a half-folded photograph. He held it up in front of Bastien.

"A picture is worth a thousand words."

Bastien glared at the faded photograph and, for a moment, he forgot about everything else. He couldn't deny what he saw with his own eyes: his father, young and smiling, with his arm around Olivier's shoulders. It looked like they were at some sort of party together.

"They were happier days." Olivier placed the photograph down on his desk. "Your father didn't approve of my ideas or growing ambitions though, and he especially hated when I started working with my team of writers. He found it insulting, believing I bought my success. I suppose he'd be turning in his grave if he ever heard I'd resorted to kidnapping writers. All the same, it's quite amusing that his only moderately successful story was half-written by a woman."

"That woman was my mother!" Bastien clenched his fists. He thought not just of her, but of Charlotte and

Alice and Theo's mother; strong, talented women who'd carved out their own paths in life. "My parents had more talent in their little fingers than you could ever dream of. None of your books belong to you."

"As long as it has my name on the cover, I don't care." Olivier shrugged. "Soon, Olivier Odieux will be the only name that matters."

"A story isn't worth anything if it's not told from the heart," said Bastien. "The words mean nothing if you don't feel every single one."

Olivier scoffed. "You sound just like your father. A fool to the end. Matters of the heart are a waste of time. Look where it got your parents – up in flames."

Bastien bit down on his lip; Olivier wasn't worthy of his tears.

"What did they find out? What else are you planning?"

Olivier shook his head, his wide shoulders bouncing up and down. "That doesn't concern you."

"You're just a coward." Bastien wanted his words to crawl under Olivier's skin. "You let your brothers do all of your dirty work while you hide in your gilded mansion. You hide behind the words of other writers. You don't even have the courage to tell me the truth. You're a fraud."

Olivier frowned. "Make no mistake that I'm the one in charge. My books are only the beginning of it all." He walked over to the bookcases and ran his wrinkled hands across the shelves. "He who controls the words controls the world."

"So you want to control the world?" Bastien's voice was hoarse, his throat scratchy like sandpaper. "For a thief and a murderer, world domination is a little ambitious."

"I'm much more than that," Olivier said, his voice booming. "Your parents thought that words were freedom. But I know the truth. Words can scare and incite. Words can dominate and rule. As will I."

Bastien stared at Olivier, his mouth wide open. "What are you planning to do?"

Olivier smiled, running his hand through his thinning hair. "It's simple really. The only stories that matter will be mine. The only voice that matters will be *mine*. I alone will rule, not just by the sword, but by the pen. I will restore order and leadership to this country."

Bastien scoffed. Did Olivier really believe the words flying out of his mouth? He sounded like an old king with his arms wrapped around a throne that was no longer his. "That will never happen."

Olivier loomed over Bastien, his wispy hair brushing against his cheeks. Bastien wanted to look away but he held the man's gaze, looking right into Olivier's empty eyes.

"Visionaries can't exist without belief. And I have absolute belief in myself." Olivier clapped his hands and stood up sharply. "Now, I think it's time to get rid of this notebook once and for all."

Bastien thrashed wildly, the chair rocking with the force of his movements. All that was left was to plead, no matter how much it pained him. "Please, I'm begging you."

"Begging is unbelievably distasteful." Olivier tutted and patted his dressing-gown pocket. "Ah, my matches must still be in my bedroom. I'll be back. I trust you won't move." He winked as he left the room, his shuffling footsteps descending the stairs.

Bastien thrashed harder. The chair creaked as it swayed and the rope dug deeper into his skin. He had to get out of here. He couldn't bear to watch his notebook, the last thing he had of his parents, turn to ashes, especially not now when he knew there were secrets inside. He had to stop Olivier, but how could he when he was tied to a chair? Bastien brought his hands to his mouth and started chewing the rope. It was all he could do.

Then a cold sharp breeze made the hair on the back of his neck stand up. It was followed by a quiet, mumbling sound: the sound of the city waking up outside. Bastien paused. The window behind him was now open…and he had the strange sense that someone was just beyond it.

"It's me." Theo's voice rang out as clearly as the bells of the Sacré-Cœur.

"You're okay!" Bastien tried to turn in the chair. "How in the name of Saint-Germain did you get up here?"

A percussion of thumps and bumps followed, and then Theo was standing in front of Bastien, his hair resembling a bird's nest and a toothy grin plastered on his face. "I climbed up the balconies."

"You climbed?" Bastien couldn't believe it. The boy afraid of heights had scaled an entire building just to save him. "How did you get away?"

"Louis and Monsieur Xavier got into a fight." Another quick smile flashed across Theo's face. "For an older man, Louis is pretty strong. As for the climbing, I guess I just thought about you in danger. I didn't stop to think about the height." Theo's eyes darted around the room. "Speaking of danger, where is Olivier?"

"Gone to get matches. He's going to burn my notebook. Can you find something to cut me free?"

"Oh right, yes. Sorry." Theo opened the desk drawer and, after a moment of rummaging, pulled out a long letter opener. "This should do."

"What about Sami?" Bastien asked. "Is he okay?"

Theo hesitated as he cut away at the rope. "He got away before I did. I'm not sure where he went. I think he called out that he was going to get help, but it was all so dark and confusing down there."

Panic fluttered in Bastien's chest, but only for a moment. He knew Sami wouldn't abandon them, not now when they were so close. He hoped he was heading back to the orphanage to lead everyone here.

The rope around Bastien's wrists and ankles fell away. "You did it!" He jumped to his feet. "Let's get out of here." He raced over to the fireplace and grabbed his notebook.

Heavy footsteps trudged up the staircase. Olivier was coming back.

Theo scrambled back onto the window sill. "Hurry!"

Fuelled by adrenaline and fear, Bastien grabbed the

295

photograph of his father from the desk and jumped up onto the sill. Theo was already edging along the balcony outside, towards the end of the window ledge.

The door flung open and Olivier entered the study. He glanced at the fireplace and turned to Bastien, his teeth grinding as he spoke. "So, you've chosen to die. So be it."

"You're wrong. I choose to live."

Bastien didn't wait for a reply. He climbed through the window into the morning light, and slammed it shut behind him. A little further along the balcony, Theo looked down. His face froze with fear.

"What's the matter?" Bastien called.

It was at that exact moment that he smelled the smoke. He followed Theo's gaze and looked down.

Below his feet were flames.

32
ON THE ROOFTOPS OF MONTMARTRE

The frosty wind carried the smoke from the flames higher, curling its way into their lungs.

"What happened?" Bastien stared down at the blaze that had engulfed the ground floor of Olivier's house.

"I don't know," Theo said. "There were no flames when I escaped from the cellar. Maybe Monsieur Xavier started a fire? Louis could be in trouble!"

Bastien's heart skipped a beat for Louis. Even though he'd been pulled into evil schemes by his brothers, he had done the right thing by returning Bastien's notebook. He was a good person; he'd just lost sight of who he was. Bastien hoped he had managed to escape.

As they stood trapped on the narrow balcony with

no clear escape, Bastien refused to meet the same fate as his parents. He was going to survive. They both were. His resolve was made of steel and grit.

"We have to go up." Bastien pointed to the rooftop. "It's the only option."

"The rooftop?" Theo gulped. "Surely we should be looking for a way down, not *up*?"

Bastien looked out across Montmartre and the rest of Paris. A light layer of frost covered the rooftops like icing sugar. From such a height, the city looked like it had been drawn in squiggly lines by a young child; it didn't feel real. But Bastien was all too aware of just how real the distance between him and the ground was.

"It's too dangerous. The flames are rising." Bastien turned away from the fire and looked up. Just above their heads, halfway between them and the rooftop, a large stone gargoyle face jutted out from the wall. Bastien shivered. It was another one of Olivier's obscene decorations, but it gave him an idea. "We can use that as a foothold to climb. And then maybe we can find another way down from the roof."

The windowpane rattled behind them. Bastien didn't look back. He didn't want to ever look at Olivier again.

"We have to move now."

"I can't do it." Theo flattened against the wall. His breaths were panicked, sharp and shallow.

"We have to. It's our only option."

"I can't. You know I can't."

"You just climbed up two balconies to save me!" Bastien shuffled closer to Theo. "You can do this."

"That was different." Theo's voice shook. "This is much, much higher."

Bastien knew Theo was thinking of his parents and how he'd sworn to always keep his feet firmly on the ground.

"You've helped me to be brave when I needed it the most." Bastien squeezed Theo's shoulder. "Let me help you. Nothing bad will happen if you trust me. I promise."

"Okay." Theo's smile was only half convincing. "But you go first."

Bastien scrambled up onto the stone face, which gave him just enough room to stand. It was slippery under his feet and he carefully stretched, finding purchase on the drainpipe that ran along the top edge of the building. With a final burst of energy, he pulled himself up and rolled onto the rooftop in a tangle of tired arms and aching legs.

Staying low, Bastien crawled onto his stomach and peered over the edge. The flames had already reached the second-floor balcony. He held his hand out to Theo. "Just focus on my voice."

Theo followed every move that Bastien had made with scientific precision. He climbed onto the stone face and waited the exact same number of seconds before standing on his tiptoes to grab hold of the drainpipe. Then he stretched the tips of his fingers until they brushed Bastien's cold hands.

"Bravo! Almost there." Bastien tightened his grip around Theo's wrists and heaved him up onto the rooftop beside him.

They sat for a moment, their breath coming back to them. Sitting on top of a burning building was a first for them both.

"What now?"

Bastien stood and walked to the opposite edge of the building. The neighbouring roof was just over a metre away, its black weathervane peeking out from the other side of the trees that surrounded Olivier's house.

"I think we can jump across to the next roof," he said.

"Jump?" Suddenly, Theo was right beside him.

"It's not that far."

"Maybe for you!" Theo squealed. "My legs are half the length of yours."

Bastien always forgot that Theo was younger and smaller, for the wisdom he possessed doubled his height and his inventiveness stretched the bones in his arms.

"We'll jump together then," Bastien decided. "Hold my hand and don't let go under any circumstances. There's enough space for us to take a run-up. Make sure to land on your feet…not your face. Understand?"

Before Theo could reply, a cracking sound reverberated around the rooftop. They both turned. On the other side of the chimney stack, Olivier emerged from the attic hatch. His face glistened with blobs of sweat which did nothing to hide his fury.

Bastien pulled Theo behind him and they crouched down, hidden behind the stack.

"I know you're up here," Olivier spluttered. "Enough of your childish games."

Horns wailed in the distance. Bastien closed his eyes and muttered a wish for an army of police and firefighters to arrive. Had Sami managed to get back to the orphanage and lead Alice and the others here?

"We're trapped," said Theo.

"We're going to have to jump now." Bastien

straightened his back. "He'll find us any second."

Theo tried to move but his legs were bolted together. No lockpick could help him now. "I can't."

The slate tiles crunched under Olivier's heavy footsteps. He emerged from behind the chimney stack, his face a fiery menace. "You can't escape me!"

Olivier's cries forced Bastien upright. He stood tall, his fury refusing to bend. No longer would he be afraid. "You destroyed my life. You destroy everything you touch. You won't get away this time."

Suddenly, as if from nowhere, a stone landed at Bastien's feet. One hit Olivier on the shoulder and then another on the knee.

"Look! Down there!"

Bastien turned at the sound of Theo's voice. What he saw made his heart leap out of his chest: Alice, Sami and the rest of the boys from the orphanage were in the front garden, their arms full of stones and rocks. Robin sat on top of Pascal's shoulders, holding a handful of pebbles. How had Sami managed to lead them all here so quickly? Had he managed to flag down a vehicle across the city? Whatever he'd done, he had saved them.

"Leave them alone!" The wind carried Sami's voice high above the rooftops. Alice and the other boys screamed as though their lives depended on it. Well, maybe their lives didn't, but Bastien's and Theo's certainly did.

Wailing sirens and running footsteps all grew closer. Bastien spotted a group of tall figures standing in front of the gate, trying to wrench it open. Was that Charlotte and Jules? Who else was with them?

"Take aim," Alice instructed. "Fire!"

A shower of stones rained down on Olivier. His hands flew up in front of his face and suddenly, without the ability to see, he tripped over a loose slate and tumbled onto the slanted roof.

Bastien turned to Theo. This was their moment. "It's now or never."

Theo gripped his hand tight and nodded.

Together they took a few steps back and looked at each other, their smiles lifting the fear that had encased them.

"On three," said Bastien. "*Un. Deux. Trois.*"

Their feet pounded against the tiles and then the rooftop disappeared from under them and Bastien and Theo were sailing through the air. Their friendship sprouted wings. This was what it meant to have a true friend. To live a life untethered, not knowing where you might land, but to be unafraid. The wind slapped their faces and the tops of the trees brushed against the soles of Bastien's feet. Even when they landed on the neighbouring rooftop, their hands were still welded tight together.

33

HANDCUFFS AND GOODBYES

Bastien watched the police escort Olivier and Xavier Odieux away from the wreckage of the house, their hands tied behind their backs. The firefighters had arrived just in time and doused the rising flames before they'd reached the attic. Looking at the charred skeleton of Olivier's house and the unrecognizable rubble strewn across the front garden that had once been fine paintings and golden chandeliers, Bastien felt a pang of guilt. But as quick as it came, it disappeared. So what if Olivier's house had burned to the ground and everything he owned, melted away? It was what he deserved.

Bastien and Theo sat on the edge of the fountain, their shoulders draped in a blanket that a kind policewoman had given them. They'd been rescued from the next-door rooftop by the police and led through the house that belonged to Olivier's neighbour, an old, bemused woman dripping in diamonds and furs, who'd been listening to her gramophone and not heard a single thing.

"So what happens now?" Bastien asked the policewoman.

"Now we collect every piece of evidence we can find to build our case against the Odieux family. Your friend Sami provided us with the catacomb location. As we speak, he's leading our team of officers to the writers. You boys have been so brilliantly brave."

"What about my parents?" As happy as Bastien was that the writers would soon return to their families, the question of justice for his parents was still unanswered.

"That case depends on the evidence and subsequent investigations." The policewoman squeezed Bastien's shoulder. "We've passed your statement along to the Cannes police, about Xavier Odieux admitting to starting the fire on behalf of Olivier. That's all we can do for now. I'm very sorry I can't offer you more, but we'll be in touch as soon as we hear anything."

Perhaps the happily-ever-after of fairy tales was a

stretch too far for Bastien. In a world without his parents, all that was left for him was a happy-for-now. Would the confession be enough to keep Monsieur Xavier and Olivier behind bars? What if he couldn't get justice, even now, for his parents? He tried not to dwell on it.

A furious cry ripped the morning sky in two.

"This isn't over!" Olivier thrashed in the grip of a burly policeman, his eyes set on Bastien like an archer observing his target. "Your days are numbered, Bastien Bonlivre. I swear it!"

The policeman bundled Olivier into the car and Bastien looked away. He hoped Olivier would be behind bars for a very long time so that he couldn't hurt him, or anyone he cared about, ever again. The man would have trouble plotting his domination in the confines of a cell.

The police car belched into life and reversed back down the street. It grew smaller, turning into a blue blob in the distance. Bastien watched until it disappeared from view.

"Bastien! Theo!" Alice ran at them. Her hug was so powerful it almost knocked both of them into the fountain. "Are you okay?"

Theo jumped down, brushed off his trousers and

gave Alice his most convincing smile. "I'm absolutely fine. Just another day in Paris."

"I'm not so sure," Bastien admitted. His body and mind were scrambled, as though he'd lived a hundred lives in one day. "I'm so glad you came. I knew you wouldn't let us down."

Alice squeezed his hand. "When you didn't turn up I knew something was wrong. Thank goodness Sami came back and told us what had happened. I just can't believe it…" She sniffed and wiped away her tears. "Will you come back to Le Chat Curieux? My parents have taken the rest of the boys there for breakfast. Maman said they needed feeding after all that hard work throwing stones. That kind policewoman said she'd give us a lift."

"Will you wait for me?" Bastien asked. "I need to say goodbye to someone first."

"Of course." Alice looped her arm through Theo's. "We'll wait for you by the gate."

Louis hid in the shadows of the trees that lined Olivier's lawn. He'd fled from the burning house into the garden, and even when the police arrived, he'd stayed put. His trousers were singed and his coat was covered in flecks of ash but his face lit up as Bastien walked towards him.

"How joyful it is to see you're okay! I couldn't quite bear to face my brothers, nor the police. I was hoping to sneak away, but I couldn't go until I was sure you were safe."

"Your brothers are gone," Bastien replied. He looked Louis up and down. "What exactly happened between you and Xavier? How did the fire start?"

Louis fiddled with his coat sleeve. "It all happened so quickly. We got into a fight down in the cellar. I still know how to push his buttons. Xavier was just about to throw your dear friends into the oubliette when I pulled him back by his cloak. We almost fell in ourselves. I grabbed one of the candles on the wall…I only meant to warn him off but I lost my grip and that was it." Louis paused for breath. "I was too slow to stop the fire spreading."

"You did what you had to do," Bastien said. "You helped save us."

"I could've saved many more people if I'd acted sooner. The writers…" A sob caught in his throat. "And your parents."

Bastien looked at Louis and saw him for who he truly

was: a kind soul who had lost his own way amongst the wickedness of his brothers. "Don't blame yourself for things that have already happened," he said. "You finally did the right thing, standing up to them. It can't be easy to turn away from family."

Louis coughed into his handkerchief. "Blood isn't always thicker than water. I was becoming far too old to blindly follow my brothers."

Bastien thought of Theo and Sami. They were like brothers to him, but he was certain that he'd follow them anywhere if they needed him.

"You should go," he said. "Before the police find you."

Louis glanced over Bastien's shoulder and sank further back into the trees. "I think it will do me some good to leave this city behind." His thoughts drifted far away to Philippe, the two of them in the mountains together, with nothing but a roaring fire and the type of love that kept you warm during the coldest winter. Perhaps a new type of life was possible, after all.

Louis stuck out his hand and Bastien stepped forward to shake it. "You're a credit to your parents. I hope you get the justice for them that they deserve."

Tears swelled in Bastien's eyes as he thought of his

mother sitting at her writing desk, and his father drinking coffee straight from the pot as he read over his day's work. Bastien would relive the tragedy of their loss for the rest of his life, but he hoped that, day by day, the sadness would grow quieter, like a fading record that had been played one too many times.

"*Prenez-soins de vous.*" Louis turned and walked further into the trees.

"Take care, too." Bastien waved, before turning towards the gates in search of his friends.

Bastien stepped into the warmth of Le Chat Curieux and followed the noise, walking with Alice and Theo through the adjoining corridor from the bookshop to the café. Sami and the boys had gathered every chair and pulled the tables together, which were piled with fresh baguettes, pots of strawberry, apricot and fig jam, and jugs of Charlotte's infamous *chocolat chaud*. Behind the café counter, Charlotte and Jules loaded pastries onto another plate.

"Look who's here!" Sami shouted.

The boys cheered and jumped to their feet, drowning Bastien and Theo in hugs.

"Come sit down." Alice led Bastien to a chair at the head of the table. "You must be starving."

Bastien's stomach grumbled on cue. Last night's dinner felt so long ago. He sat down next to Sami and Clément and reached for a croissant.

"I could've taken Monsieur Xavier out by myself," Clément said. "But well done all the same." He turned to Alice and flexed his left bicep. "I used to sneak into the boxing gym off the Place de la Concorde."

Alice rolled her eyes and slurped on her spoonful of thick hot chocolate.

"How happy I am to see you!" Bastien turned to Sami, who held a mug of steaming mint tea. His father's Croix de Guerre was pinned to his collar, freshly polished. "Thank you for getting back to the orphanage and leading the police to Olivier's house. Did they rescue the writers?"

Sami smiled. "Take a moment to breathe, Bastien! I managed to flag down a lift." He took a small sip. "I told the taxi driver it was urgent police business and that seemed to do the trick. The police got to the writers just in time, but they were in a bad way. I don't think they'd eaten a proper meal in days."

The guilt Bastien had felt for leaving the writers

behind stung him again. Sami saw it on his face.

"They need to rest and recover, but the police said they will be fine."

Sami's reassuring words were as calming as a sip of hot tea. Bastien thought of Jacques Joli, Delphine de la Reine and the other writers. They would all be reunited with their families.

Suddenly, hands wrapped around Bastien's waist and lifted him into the air. He dropped his half-eaten croissant.

"How glad we are to see you safe!" Jules boomed.

"Thank you for believing Alice." Bastien steadied himself as Jules planted him back on the ground. "But I'm sorry I wasn't honest earlier. I was too scared to involve you until I was sure of Monsieur Xavier's guilt. I couldn't have let anything happen to you both."

"I knew something was amiss from the moment we visited you at the orphanage." Charlotte swept him into a hug. Her checked dress smelled of apples and cinnamon. "To think of what that awful man put you through..."

Jules adjusted his glasses. He tried to turn away but Bastien noticed the teardrops forming under the lenses.

"It's no one's fault," Bastien replied. "At least we're all free of Monsieur Xavier now. And Olivier…" Bastien thought of the photograph in his pocket, the one he'd stolen from the study. "Did you ever hear of my father being friends with Olivier?"

Charlotte and Jules exchanged a look between them. They both shook their heads. "Your father never mentioned that man. Not once, not even in passing." Jules removed his glasses to wipe his eyes. "He was always incredibly kind about other authors. Neither of your parents ever said a bad word about anyone."

"Put that to the back of your mind for now." Charlotte kissed his cheek and squeezed his hand. "You're safe. Now, please eat."

Bastien sat back down and reached for another croissant, almond this time. He listened to the buzz of the conversations around him: Theo and Alice were discussing the mechanics of an automatic rock-launcher and Sami was telling the rest of the boys about the different types of fish he used to sell at the market alongside his father.

It wasn't quite how he'd imagined all of this would end, but, looking around the café, surrounded by his friends, Bastien realized something true. He knew that if his world ever fell to pieces again, he had a whole troupe of loving, loyal musketeers who would gladly answer his call for help.

34

A NEW LIFE

After the events in the catacombs and Montmartre, Bastien swore that life would get better, and he'd no longer dwell on the past.

It did and he didn't. Not always, at least.

After a couple of days of government interviews, the orphanage had been placed under new management and the first thing that the new director, Madame Gentille, had done was to break every lock and throw away each key that had kept the boys inside. Paris was their city and they deserved to experience all it had to offer, every single day.

Madame Gentille was a tall woman with hair the colour of mercury and a heart-shaped face, as though she'd been kind and full of love from the moment she was born. More creativity and more freedom was her mantra. "Each of you have your own unique talents," she'd announced on the first morning of her arrival. "The greatest gift is to share them with each other."

Theo set up his own workshop in the cellar, and every afternoon he taught the boys how to make things with their hands. Under Theo's skilful eye, they carved wooden figurines, which they used to put on shows, Timothée directing with his usual flair and enthusiasm. Felix's new guitar provided the musical accompaniment.

Every evening, the boys escaped to the library room. Monsieur Xavier's old office was now a room full of paper-made happiness; from floor to ceiling, books covered every surface. Bastien was given a storyteller's armchair and every night he sat down and told tales, old and new, to his ever-adoring audience.

As for Sami, he'd gone to the director's office, Bastien and Theo by his side, and told her everything, from his journey to France in search of his father to his attempts to get back home. He'd found his voice again and this time he was heard. Madame Gentille immediately launched into action and pestered government officials for days on end, scheduling regular meetings and long phone calls until they could no longer ignore her demands.

Her efforts were rewarded with a government grant, just enough to cover Sami's passage back home, and Madame Gentille told him the news at dinner, a week after he'd first told her his story. His ticket home was booked for the first of January.

"I'm going home," Sami had cried, as the boys gathered round, suffocating him with hugs. "Finally."

The remaining days leading up to Christmas were busy with change. All traces of Monsieur Xavier were wiped clean from the east wing and Bastien took special pleasure in pulling down his creepy portrait and breaking it up in the courtyard, the others cheering him on. Clément picked up the wooden pieces and threw them into the roaring furnace in the dormitory. In the portrait's place, Madame Gentille lined the hall with red ribbons and pine tree wreaths, and she placed a grand tree in the dormitory. Underneath the furnace, she placed a pair of shoes for every boy, where they would receive presents, even for those who didn't celebrate Christmas.

Le Réveillon, the grand, sumptuous feast of Christmas Eve, arrived with high expectations. Madame Gentille promised the boys an evening to be remembered; excitable whispers of roast chicken, lobster, garlic-buttered snails and mountains of creamy potatoes travelled round the orphanage all day. There'd even been mention of thirteen different desserts, as Madame Gentille was from Provence where it was a tradition – one that all the boys heartily approved of. Timothée was certain he'd seen Chef carrying crates of dough, fresh fruit and chocolate nougat through the gates.

"Are you coming to eat?" Theo stood at the dormitory door, dressed in his most festive knitted jumper.

"I'll join you soon." Bastien was sprawled across his bed, brow furrowed in concentration. Even the smells from the kitchen couldn't pull him away. "I'm working."

Theo walked over and tapped Bastien's head. "You need to give your eyes a rest."

Bastien's notebook was open, surrounded by library books and scraps of paper. Since Montmartre, he'd spent every free moment poring over the pages in his notebook, trying to figure out what secret it might contain. He couldn't concentrate on anything else. What had his parents known about Olivier? What was in here that had cost them their lives? He'd read the only sentence his parents had scribbled on the first page a thousand times, rearranging the letters in different orders to see if anything would uncover a secret message.

"Once upon a time, there were three musketeers destined for a great adventure."

But there was no meaning in those sixty-three letters, nothing that made sense.

He'd flipped the notebook upside down and shaken it, but there was nothing. No secret note. No hollowed cover that revealed a hidden clue. All that was in there was that single sentence and his own scribbles from his story of the missing writers.

"I don't understand." Bastien rolled onto his back and stared up at the ceiling. "Olivier was so desperate to get his hands on my notebook, but there's nothing in here about him. What am I missing?"

Theo picked up the notebook and looked at the photograph of Olivier with Bastien's father that was tucked inside. "Have you ever considered that Olivier just got it wrong? He was a paranoid, delusional man. You can't torture yourself looking for answers that aren't there, Bastien. Focus on finishing your story for LeGrand. Focus on the things you can control."

"I know." Bastien sighed. "But you should've seen the look on his face. He was so fixated on destroying the notebook. He told me that he would control the world with words. What if he's still planning something else? The thing that's so terrible he had my parents killed to conceal it! I need to know what it is."

"Boys! Dinner is served!" Madame Gentille's dinner call floated up the staircase and into the dormitory.

Theo pulled Bastien to his feet. "Olivier is in prison. He can't hurt you or do anything to anyone while he's in there. Whatever his plan was, he can't carry it out. Now, come on. There'll be no food left if we don't hurry."

Bastien put his belongings back in his trunk and followed Theo downstairs, where a veritable feast was waiting for them in the dining hall. Plates of food covered the table, from a glistening goose and oysters with lemon wedges to roasted figs, marzipan drops and slabs of nougat, drizzled in honey and pistachio crumbs.

Theo turned to Bastien, his eyes wide with delight and his tongue lolling like a puppy's. "Grab two of everything!"

Bastien stacked his plate high and took his seat at the dining table. Cheerful chaos was all around him; Pascal was carefully dissecting each morsel of food, savouring each bite and describing every taste in detail; Sami was helping Robin fork roast goose onto his plate, while Clément and Timothée were competing with Fred and Felix to see how many potatoes they could each fit in their mouths at one time.

"Tonight we'll eat until our bellies are full!" Theo shouted, his mouth already stuffed with roast goose.

The boys roared and clunked their cups of sparkling apple juice against the table. Madame Gentille, who sat at the head of the table next to a smiling Chef, raised her wine glass to them all. "Dig in! Eat until you can no longer stand."

As Bastien ate and chatted, his mind quietened and the questions about his notebook that plagued him slipped away. He told himself he didn't always have to worry about the unknown. Happiness could still exist after hardship.

Happiness was a full belly and a room full of people you love.

A week later...Sunday 31ˢᵗ December, 1922

"**G**ive me my bow tie back, you Camembert-gobbler!"

"It's mine. Get your own."

Timothée flew through the air like a cat tracking a bird and landed on top of Pascal's bed. He grabbed the bow tie and raced from the dormitory, his laughter echoing down the staircase.

"Come along, all of you." Madame Gentille stood at the dormitory door in a black ankle-length gown. "The invitation said to be there by seven o'clock. You know how important it is to be punctual."

Tonight they were off to the Hôtel Ritz. LeGrand was hosting a New Year's Eve party. He'd invited Bastien and the rest of the boys to come and dance the night away.

Bastien laced up his smart black shoes and reached under his bed, grabbing his new green notebook, a Christmas gift from Madame Gentille. He hadn't wanted to part with his parents' notebook and so he had decided to write his story for LeGrand in his new one.

Between Christmas and New Year, Bastien had barely paused for breath. But tonight he would deliver his story. Then he could focus on all of the unanswered questions about his parents and Olivier that he'd pushed to the back of his mind.

Madame Gentille hurried them out of the orphanage and led the way through the city. All of the boys walked in pairs apart from Bastien, Theo and Sami, who huddled together at the back.

"I can't believe this is our last night together," said Bastien as they crossed the Pont Neuf.

Sami slowed his pace. "I'll miss you both, but I can't wait to see my mother and Leïla." A smile, the width of an ocean, spread across his face.

"What joy," Theo replied, "to be reunited with the ones you love."

Bastien nodded in agreement. Sami had been through so much, but Bastien couldn't deny the twinge of jealousy that quickly passed through him. He wished he could see his parents again, one more time.

They walked past the Louvre and headed down Rue Saint-Honoré. The street was busy, people rushing in and out of shops to buy last-minute outfits and New Year's gifts. Bastien breathed in the promise that tonight held; the sight of his city in all its glory cheered him. At one time, he thought he might not ever see it again. He was glad to be free.

They heard the Hôtel Ritz before they saw it. As they entered the square, the sound of music and people laughing and chatting at the top of their lungs hit them like a wave. Madame Gentille quickened her pace and the boys doubled their stride to keep up.

"Please be on your best behaviour." She whipped out her handkerchief and wiped a blob of melted chocolate from Pascal's mouth. "Remember to thank Monsieur LeGrand for having you here tonight."

The doorman opened the hotel's gilded doors and the boys followed the director. Stepping into the lobby, Bastien was mesmerized by the sight of luxury that oozed from every corner. Marble columns lined the lobby hall where a sweeping staircase curled upwards. Rich mahogany tables and chairs stood upon gold patterned carpets.

"*Bonsoir.*" A line of waiters and waitresses snaked down the hallway towards the restaurant doors. "The party is this way. Eat and drink and dance as much as you want!"

Timothée looked at one of the waitresses suspiciously. "And we don't have to pay for it?"

She laughed. "No, it's all free."

Timothée raced through the restaurant door, Pascal and Clément snapping at his heels.

"This is the best night of my life!"

Even at seven o'clock, the party was already in full swing. Paris attracted people from all over the world and Bastien heard American, Spanish, Italian and Irish voices. A jazz band were playing on a stage and the tables and chairs had been pushed to the edge of the restaurant to create a makeshift dance floor. People danced, holding hands and twirling each other. Waitresses slipped between them, balancing silver trays loaded with sparkling drinks and finger food.

In the corner, Bastien saw Alice in a puffy rose-coloured dress. Charlotte and Jules were by the dance floor, talking with Delphine de la Reine. Alice spotted him and ran over.

"Isn't this brilliant? I can't believe the Mitchell Jazz Kings are playing tonight!" Alice tapped her foot in time to the trumpets.

"You look like a macaron," Bastien laughed.

"*Don't*. Maman made me wear this dress." Alice pouted.

Theo cleared his throat. "I think you look *jolie*."

"I know I look pretty." Alice grinned wickedly. "But thank you. You scrub up well yourself."

Bastien looked around and found what he was looking for: a familiar black trilby hat poking out of a crowd. He needed to do this before his courage disappeared.

"I'm going to go and give my story to LeGrand." He fidgeted in his dinner jacket. Suddenly, it felt too big for him.

"He'll love it." Theo hugged him tight.

"And if he doesn't, then he's the biggest fool in this place," Alice added. "Come on, Theo, I want to see Sami before he leaves tomorrow."

Bastien navigated his way through the restaurant. He squeezed through gaps on the dance floor and narrowly avoided waiters with loaded trays. He kept his eyes on the trilby hat bobbing above the crowd, and finally found LeGrand next to the buffet table.

"I'm so glad you could make it." LeGrand put down his plate and shook Bastien's hand.

"Thank you for inviting us."

"Of course. It wouldn't be a party without the heroes of the hour."

Bastien felt his cheeks warming; he didn't feel like a hero. He reached into his jacket pocket and held out his green notebook. "Sorry it's a bit later than expected."

LeGrand handled the notebook with care. "Nonsense, my boy. It's quite understandable, especially after everything you've been through. What a feat to have written a story during it all." He sat down and indicated for Bastien to do the same.

"Might I ask what your story is about?"

"It's about a loyal troupe of musketeers who find themselves on a most unexpected journey."

"I can't wait to read it." LeGrand slipped the notebook into his jacket pocket. "How are you holding up?"

"I'm finding it hard to shut my brain off." Bastien fiddled with his cuffs. "Sometimes I can distract myself, but normally all I can think about is everything that happened. There's still so much I don't know about Olivier. About my parents."

"I read the full report about what happened in the news. Olivier Odieux has always been a disgrace, but to kidnap writers and to be accused of your parents' murder…" A look of disgust appeared on LeGrand's face. "Well, he's sunk further than I ever could have imagined."

Bastien baulked at LeGrand's words. It was more than just an accusation; Olivier had killed his parents. He hoped the police would gather enough evidence to prove his and Monsieur Xavier's guilt.

"Do you know Olivier?"

LeGrand shook his head. "We met a few times at parties a few years ago, only in passing. He always loved himself. You could tell from a glance that he thought he was a god."

Flashes of Olivier's comments passed through Bastien's mind. *He who controls the words controls the world.*

"Olivier said my father betrayed him, but he didn't say why."

LeGrand frowned. "I wasn't aware that Hugo even knew Olivier. They couldn't have been more different. Not just as writers, but as people."

"That's what I don't understand." Despite the beautiful party that surrounded him, Bastien felt his thoughts spiralling once again. "Maybe he just wanted my parents out of the way? They were such talented writers, after all."

LeGrand put a hand on Bastien's shoulder. "Don't make yourself sadder, my dear boy. Try and enjoy your evening. Your parents wouldn't want you to spend the rest of your life in torment over things you cannot change. The past is already written, but your future is a blank page and a fresh fountain pen."

LeGrand was right, but Bastien also knew that his parents wouldn't have turned away from a mystery. If there were questions still unanswered, they would have hunted down the truth like a pair of hounds. He would do the same.

"I just wish I'd asked them more about their past while I still had the chance," Bastien replied.

LeGrand plucked a pen from his jacket lining and scribbled something on a napkin. "If you're delving into the past, then I know someone who might be able to help. Pauline Savoir is the Head Archivist at the Mazarin Library. Has been for the last twenty years. If you're looking for something, then chances are she'll find it for you."

"*Merci.*" Bastien took the napkin and slipped it into his suit pocket. He didn't know whether an archivist would be able to tell him much about his parents, or how well his father had truly known Olivier, but he was grateful for LeGrand's help all the same.

"Now, let's go and ring in the New Year." LeGrand pulled Bastien up and towards the dance floor. "There's plenty of brilliant people here I'd like you to meet."

After gathering in the square to watch the fireworks light up the night sky, Bastien's eyes began to flicker with fatigue. A little after midnight, Madame Gentille and the boys said their goodbyes and went home. Bastien crawled into his bed, not even bothering to change out of his suit.

In the bed next to him, Sami yawned. "I hope this year is a better one for you, Bastien."

He smiled silently in the dark. "I hope so too. *Bonne nuit*." Bastien turned in his bed, pulled the blanket up to his neck and closed his eyes.

Bastien always took longer to fall asleep than the others, and so he told himself a story in his head, in which his parents came back to him.

The story soothed him to sleep quicker than any lullaby.

FAREWELL TO A FRIEND

Standing beneath the clock tower outside the Gare de Lyon the next morning, Bastien blinked back a tear. As sad as he was to see Sami leave, he was grateful for the chance to say farewell. Bastien knew all too well how precious goodbyes were. Like much else in life, they weren't guaranteed. To look a friend in the eye and tell them how much they would be missed was a privilege.

The other boys had said their farewells that morning, while Bastien had gone to Le Chat Curieux to pick up a bag full of croissants for Sami's long journey.

The station was busy with Parisians eagerly rushing to their next destination. Bastien watched the crowds of people weaving in and out of each other. He watched parents juggling suitcases between them while little children fought at their feet; a group of old men outside the kiosk playing a fierce game of chess; people hugging each other goodbye and waving from the platform as a train slowly crept out of the station, onwards to its next stop.

And he spotted Sami, battling against the tide of the crowd, with a ticket clenched tightly in one hand and a battered suitcase in the other.

"All set?" Bastien asked.

Sami nodded. A long journey was ahead. He would have to take the train through the Pyrénées and into Spain. He'd reach the port town of Algeciras and cross the sea, docking in Tangier. Sami planned to find a ride down the coast from there, but he'd make the week-long journey back to his city by foot if necessary. He'd run the entire way if it led him back to his family.

They walked to platform five, where Sami's train awaited him.

"The orphanage won't be the same without you." Bastien tried not to let his sadness show. "We'll all miss you. I'll miss you a lot."

Sami made a strange gurgling sound, as if he was choking on an apple core. He couldn't find the words to say how thankful he was that Bastien had helped him to believe in the goodness of people once again. It was worth opening up to people in life, to make the type of friend who would be there for you no matter what.

The words refused to come out and so instead, Sami put down his suitcase and swept Bastien into a hug.

"Thank you for everything."

"Likewise." Bastien choked back the wobble in his throat and passed the suitcase to Sami.

"Make sure you write to me!" Sami called as he boarded the train and turned into the carriage.

"Wait!" Theo's voice cut through the entire station, louder than the train engine. Bastien turned and spotted Theo sprinting down the platform. "Wait for me!"

The shrill whistle of the train sounded and a burly ticket inspector motioned for Bastien to move back from the platform's edge. Theo skidded to a halt at his side.

"I'm too late, aren't I? Clément had me working on his boxing gloves all morning and I completely lost track of time. Is—"

Bastien laughed. "*Calme-toi*. He's just got on. You can still catch him."

334

The engine spluttered an oily cough, and the train lurched into life. The carriage window rolled down and Sami's head popped out.

"You made it!" Sami grinned at Theo. He saluted, his father's medal glittering brightly on his jacket. Just like his father, Sami was a brave soldier. He'd survived the unthinkable and now he was on his way back home to find peace, at last.

"I wouldn't have missed it for the world!" Theo called back. "Safe travels, *mon ami*."

"I'll see you both again one day," Sami called.

"*Bon voyage!*" Bastien and Theo ran down the length of the platform until it came to an end. They watched the train until it turned into a pea on the horizon. Then they turned and walked back through the station.

"We will see Sami again, won't we?" Theo looked at Bastien.

All Bastien could do was nod and hope he was right. True friends, the irreplaceable type, were as rare as green diamonds. He knew you had to hold onto them as tightly as possible with both hands. But he also knew that you had to let them go when their own story pulled them in another direction.

They exited the station and Theo checked the time on the clock tower. "We've still got another hour until we need to be back for lunch."

Bastien looked around at the people rushing past him. The city was his to explore again, but there was still a voice in his head, the one that reappeared whenever he felt himself relax. It told him that he wasn't yet safe, not when there was still a supposed secret in his possession that Olivier had killed to protect.

"Earth to Bastien!" Theo's voice snapped him out of his daze and the voice quietened to a mere whisper. Olivier was sitting in a jail cell, awaiting trial. Bastien was safe.

"I was just thinking about all the things we could do in one hour," he said.

Theo jumped, clapping with glee. "Like go to the market at Place Maubert and get an almond and orange gâteau for tonight's dessert?"

"That is exactly why you're my best friend." Bastien threw his arm around Theo's shoulder.

They ran across the bridge and down the left bank of the Seine, fuelled by thoughts of sugar and the look on their friends' faces when they returned with a cake larger than most adult heads.

Bastien hadn't imagined such unlimited freedom would ever be possible again, but here he was in the heart of his city that he loved so much, roaming with his best friend. It was the sweetest taste of all.

Le Parisien

SAMEDI, 27 JANVIER 1923

THE BROTHERS ODIEUX

Today marked the first day of the "Bad Brothers" trial at the Palais de Justice, a trial that will decide the fate of infamous author, Olivier Odieux, and his younger brother, Xavier Odieux.

Since the arrest of both men in December, the case of the "Bad Brothers" has shocked and intrigued the country in equal measure. The men are said to be responsible for the kidnapping of dozens of authors, who were held against their will and forced to write for Olivier in an underground cavern deep within the catacombs. The brothers are also charged with arson, of the InterContinental Carlton Hôtel in Cannes, and the subsequent murder of beloved authors Margot and Hugo Bonlivre. At the time of his arrest, Xavier Odieux was director at the Orphanage for Gentils Garçons, where Bastien Bonlivre, the son of the victims, lives.

Bastien Bonlivre, and brave friends Theo Larouche and Sami Afriat, are credited with discovering the underground location of the kidnapped writers.

If convicted, the brothers could face a lengthy prison sentence. They strongly deny all charges.

The news of the Odieuxs' trial has brought great relief to the city, especially for members of the writing community who have lived in fear for several terrifying months as their

Quotidien

PRIX:
0 FR.30

60, RUE LA FAYETTE

TAKE THE STAND

friends and colleagues were kidnapped on the street and from their homes.

"I don't care to comment on those men or the horrors they put me through. Now is the time for healing," Delphine de la Reine, one of the kidnapped authors, said to a reporter outside her apartment. "Paris is one of the most creative, free-thinking cities in the world. Let us return to how we were before. Let us live without fear."

In an unusual turn of events, Olivier Odieux has chosen to represent himself and his brother in court. Whether this is nothing more than a publicity stunt, or a stroke of genius on the author's part, the country will watch with bated breath over the next two weeks as the fates of the two men are decided.

As both men exited the Palais de Justice, escorted by heavily-armed security, Olivier Odieux responded calmly to the probing questions from fellow journalists.

"As members of the Odieux family, such accusations against our character have always come with the territory," he said. "I'm all too familiar with plot twists, but these charges are a farce from start to finish. I have no doubt that the Odieux name will be cleared and I can continue doing what I love best: bringing my stories to life in order to change the world." ■

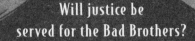

Will justice be
served for the Bad Brothers?

And can Bastien begin to write a new chapter of
his own story?

Or does Olivier still seek the secrets in
Bastien's notebook...

Find out in the next
Unexpected Adventure
from Clare Povey

COMING SOON

BASTIEN'S GLOSSARY

A born and raised Parisian, Bastien's native language is French. For those readers curious to discover the meaning behind the French words and phrases used throughout this book, here is a useful guide.

À bientôt – See you soon

À demain – See you tomorrow

Aidez-nous – Help us

Allez ! – Come on!

Bon sang ! – Good grief!

Bonne nuit – Good night

Bonsoir – Good evening

Bon voyage – Have a good trip

Ça suffit ! – That's enough!

Calme-toi ! – Calm down

Ça va ? – Are you okay?

Chocolat chaud – Hot chocolate

Chut – Ssh

Coucou / Bonjour – Hello (*Coucou* is more informal and often used as Hey there!)

D'accord – Okay

Desolé – Sorry

Écoutez ! – Listen up!

Frère – Brother

Je te promets – I promise you

Jolie – Pretty

Les potes – Mates

Mchawcha – A traditional dish from the Kabylia region in Algeria. A sweet, sugary type of thick omelette often drizzled in honey

Mon ange – My darling

Mon ami – My friend

Perdu – Lost

Petit chenapan – Little rascal

Poussons ! – Push!

Préfet – A prefect who is a representative of the French national government at a local level

Quoi ? – What?

Santé – Cheers

Tais-toi ! – Shut up!

Tirailleur – Skirmisher, a soldier involved in a short fight with a smaller number of other soldiers. The French exploited their colonized countries, recruiting thousands of men to fight as *tirailleurs* in the First World War.

Toujours – Always

Vite ! – Quickly!

Author's note

The idea for this book all started with a name. On an autumn evening in 2018, while I was working late at the office, I thought of the name Bastien Bonlivre. I chuckled and declared myself a master of puns; after all, Bonlivre [Bon livre] in French translates into Good book.

Learning another language is just like Theo's lockpick. It opens up doors and allows you to slip into other worlds. My knowledge of French gave me a name for a character and around this, I built a boy with an imagination as vast as an ocean, who believed in the power of stories not just to inform him about the world, but also to help heal the deepest of wounds.

How does a writer find their way into a story? For me, it was a combination of my love of language, asking a lot of questions and research. Research – learning and experiencing as much as I can about the world of my story – is just as important to me as writing the first sentence. I wanted Bastien to live during the 1920s. This decade in France was known as Les Années Folles – The Crazy Years – a time of great social and cultural change after the turmoil of the First World War.

Paris attracted writers, artists and creatives of every type. It was a haven for new ways of thinking, yet at the same time, extreme right-wing ideologies crept across Europe like a burglar going from house to house. I was interested in exploring the conflict between the "old" and the "new", not least because of the parallels we live in today.

When the world feels like it is falling apart, I turn to friendship. Bravery and friendship are essential elements of children's books and this story is no different. The two work alongside each other, for I have always believed that I am brave because of the brilliant friends and relationships I have made.

In *The Unexpected Tale of Bastien Bonlivre*, I wanted to write about friends who face the unexpected and bring out the best in each other. Friendship is a specific type of love that can help you to be courageous and strong, even when you don't think you have it in you.

Clare Povey, June 2021

Acknowledgements

My agent Kirsty McLachlan championed Bastien from the get-go and saw past the words that were masquerading as plot. You saw what this story could be and I am forever grateful that you took a chance on me. Thanks must also go to Dylan Sweet for thinking of the title!

Thank you to Rebecca Hill for loving my story from the very beginning; working with you has been an incredible learning experience. How lucky am I to have another brilliant editor, the indomitable Becky Walker: my story is all the better for your language wisdom and careful consideration. Thank you to Sarah Stewart for her eagle-eye copyedit and Alice Moloney and Gareth Collinson for proofreading, as well as Katharine Millichope for her incredible cover design and Sarah Cronin for making the inside look just as beautiful. Thank you to Hannah Reardon-Steward and Katarina Jovanovic for their marketing and publicity prowess; Christian Herisson and Arfana Islam for sales support; Lauren Robertson, Laura Lawrence, Penelope Mazza and the rest of the Usborne family. I'm forever grateful to you all for making my most unexpected dream come true.

Héloïse Mab. What luck it was to have you illustrate this book. You reached into my head and pulled out my characters.

Thank you to Ouissal Harize for her sensitivity read and invaluable advice on Theo's character and family background. Ouissal is a brilliant writer and she has penned pieces about the Amazigh Chaoui tribe and the women fighters in Algeria's war for independence on Middle East Eye. Check them out.

Thank you also to Fadwa for her time reading the story and offering improvements on Sami's character and the strands of Moroccan history, language and culture, while simultaneously working in a hospital during the pandemic.

Thank you to Bethan Davies, Head of Residential Care Homes UK at Action for Children for her guidance and advice on writing about children with trauma. Thanks also to Sarah Reynolds and the young people who I've worked with on writing projects at AFC. If you are able to donate, AFC are doing essential, urgent work: https://www.actionforchildren.org.uk/

Merci à Elise Wawrzyniak, ma Lilloise/Parisienne

préférée, for her expert language help. To the children I taught at École Louise Dematte and École La Tour in the village of Saint Amand Les Eaux: you inspired Bastien and his friends. Merci mille fois to Karine Delcroix, for her teaching wisdom and friendship.

Thank you to all the teachers and professors who have encouraged me throughout my studies, from comprehensive school all the way through to university. I can't list every single book and article that helped inspire and illuminate my path into this story, but a particular spotlight should shine on the following historians and writers: Emile Chabal, Olivette Otele, Lauren Elkin, Robert Darnton, Tahar Ben Jelloun, Alice Zeniter, Katherine Rundell and Brian Selznick, to name a few.

To my parents for instilling a love of reading and writing in me from an early age. From *The Adventures of Piglet* to the *Holes* fan fiction, you have always encouraged me. Thanks to my brother Matt for being nice enough to leave writing as a skill for me to master when you have managed all the other ones. To my sis-in-law Lucy and baby Flo who I hope enjoys this story when she is all grown.

To my grandparents, Rex, Tel, Marge and George. My

lovely Aunt Kerry and Uncle John, as well as Sam and Kate – my two talented cousins. Thank you to the rest of my family all over the world – from the edges of Western Australia to the lakes of New York. Your support means everything. To my extended McKie family, Gordon, James, Dave, Arlene, Jojo and Ida. And in memory of Carol and Chris, who are much missed.

Thank you to my friends, old and new, who have long indulged my ability to waffle on: Kayleigh, Georgia, Katie, Stevie, Rae, Laura, Kristen, Emily, Lizzie, Becky, Lydia, Thérèse, Chantal and Carolyn, and everyone else. I'm sorry there isn't enough space to name you all. My uni pals Sara, Megan, Becky, Alex, Samir, Oly and Jake, and the city of Sheffield for being the centre of the known universe.

Thank you to James, Katy and Ruth, my wonderful work friends, for cheering me on and not pretending to act entirely shocked when I admitted I had written a book.

Thank you to Adam. You are my best friend who helps me move through life with a lightness of touch and always reminds me that being silly is the best antidote. Je t'aimais, je t'aime, je t'aimerai.

And the biggest of thanks to you, dear readers, for picking up my book.

Share your story of reading

THE UNEXPECTED TALE OF BASTIEN BONLIVRE

@Usborne

#BastienBonlivre